PARANORM WORLD BOOK THREE
Changing Moon
A MOON SISTERS NOVEL

June Stevens Westerfield

THIS book is a work of fiction. Names, characters, places and incidents are the product of the authors' imagination or are used factiously. Any resemblance to actual persons, living or dead, business establishments, events or locales is entirely coincidental.

NO part of this book may be reproduced, scanned, or distributed in any printed or electronic form without permission. Please do not participate in or encourage piracy of copyrighted materials in violation of the author's rights. Purchase only authorized editions.

Changing Moon
Copyright ©2016 June Stevens Westerfield
All rights reserved.

ISBN: 978-1-63422-203-7
Cover Design by: Marya Heiman
Typography by: Courtney Nuckels
Editing by: Cynthia Shepp

To Lynn, you are loved and appreciated more than I could ever express. I'm happy we are family.

ONE
Jarrett

*J*ARRETT'S BODY ACHED. IT WASN'T A SHARP, STABBING pain, just a dull ache that radiated throughout his body. He felt like he had the flu—a feeling he hadn't had in over five hundred years. Opening his eyes, he blinked, grateful his eyelids didn't hurt. He could see a ceiling. When he turned his head, he took in a white wall. He was in a small, dimly lit room that smelled faintly of disinfectant and blood.

"Where...?" He tried to voice the question in his mind, but his mouth and throat were dry. All that came out was a raspy croak.

"You're in Nash City Hospital," a soothing, feminine voice said. "You're probably aching. Stay still and I'll bring you something to help with that."

He turned his head to the other side and saw a young woman in a light grey uniform rising from a chair near the bed he was laying on. The words 'Apprentice Healer' were embroidered on the top left side of the uniform tunic, with the name 'Telanna Music' underneath. She opened a door and hurried out into a well-lit hall beyond his room, leaving the door open behind her.

Jarrett fought to clear his foggy brain. Why was he in the hospital? What...? Then memories flooded his mind. *Cora laughing down at him. Anya, blood streaming down her body.*

"Anya!" he rasped, struggling to sit up. Cora was alive, and she'd slit Anya's throat. Pain that had nothing to do with the aches in his body lanced through his heart.

"Agent Campbell, please lie down." The young healer's voice sounded from the doorway, still soft, but more stern this time.

"Anya?"

He still couldn't manage more than a word at a time, but it seemed the healer understood his distress. She came to stand beside him, a kind smile beaming on her young face. Taking his hand in hers, she gave it a little squeeze. "She's just fine. She hasn't woken up yet. I'm sure you know that the body can take a little while to fully make the change."

The change. More memories flooded in. *Slitting his own wrists. Fiona and Sam's voices in the background.*

"Sure? Okay?" He coughed, struggling to sit up.

"Here, let me help you. I imagine you are still in a good deal of pain," she said, pushing two plump pillows behind his back, allowing him to sit up a little.

Healer Music moved away from him to a table near the door, returning with a large mug in her hand. "Here, drink this. It will help soothe your throat and give you a little energy."

He grasped the proffered mug and took a tentative sip. Warm pig blood slid down his throat, easing the ache. He took another drink, and the healer continued talking as she checked his pulse.

"I'm sure Miss Moon is okay. They've been sending me hourly reports for when you woke up," she said as she moved around him, touching his wrist, head, and other points, obviously doing some sort of medical scan. "We were more worried about you. By the time the two of you got here, Miss Moon was well in the middle of the change, but you were knocking at death's door. You had actually lost so much blood that we had to do a blood transfusion. You had a broken leg, and we weren't sure you'd be able to heal it on your own."

"I didn't know you could give a vampire a blood

transfusion," Jarrett said, his voice less scratchy, but not quite smooth yet. The ache in his body was starting to subside.

"You can. It's rare though. I'd never seen it done before, but we have skilled and powerful med-mages on staff, so you were in good hands."

"How long was I out?"

She ran her hands over his legs. "A little over a day. But your vitals look okay now and your leg is fully healed. How are you feeling?"

Jarrett drained the last of the blood. He could feel his strength coming back. "Better. I think I'll be a hundred percent in a little bit."

"Good. Here, have some more. It will help." She handed him another mug of blood. "You'll want to dress. We cleaned you up as much as possible, and there are some clean clothes on the chair that should fit you."

Jarrett looked down, realizing he was naked with a thin sheet as his only covering. "Oh, thanks."

The young healer smiled again, her cheeks reddening this time. "I need to go update Healer Jensen on your status. You let us know if you need anything," she said as she left.

He finished the second cup of blood. As he did, the last of his pain and weakness faded.

He dressed in the loose-fitting khaki pants and tunic that he assumed was a hospital uniform. His boots were on the floor next to the chair, so he sat and put them on. The pants were too short, barely reaching the tops of his boots.

Just as he was ready to go out and ask about seeing Anya, the door swung open and a man in a med-mage uniform walked in. He assumed it was Healer Jensen. Jarret immediately recognized him as Luca, the med-mage who had healed Anya when she'd injured her leg.

"How are you feeling?" Luca asked.

"I'm fine. My strength is back to normal," Jarrett said, standing.

"So no pain, nausea, or muscle weakness?"

"No, not at all," Jarrett said distractedly, anxious to get this over with so he could check on Anya.

Luca nodded. "Good."

If Jarrett had been paying attention, and if he hadn't felt like he deserved any and every bad thing anyone wanted to throw at him, he might have seen the fist flying at his face in time to duck. As it was, Luca's fist collided with Jarrett's chin with enough force to send him flying backward over the bed and against the wall.

Dazed, Jarrett worked his jaw. It was painful, but not broken. "Doesn't that break some 'thou shalt not harm people' oath, Doc?"

"The Hippocratic Oath stopped being administered over two hundred years ago, around the time the term *doctor* went out of style," Luca said, sneering.

"Thanks for the history lesson. Should I stand up so you can punch me again? You don't seem like the kind to kick a man while he's down," Jarrett quipped, sarcasm the only response he had. He'd get angry and put the guy through a wall, but there was no use. He'd deserved the punch. And more.

Luca sighed. "No, I'm done. And yeah, seems I do still believe in the Hippocratic Oath. But you deserved it."

Jarrett shrugged. "No argument here."

Luca ignored his response and continued. "I heard the agents say you knew the woman who kidnapped Anya, and that she hurt her as payback to you for something. I know you saved her life, but since she was in danger because of you, that doesn't mean much to me. The fact it will mean a lot to Anya is the only reason I didn't cut you into a thousand tiny pieces while you were unconscious."

Jarrett stood. "Okay."

Luca scowled. "Okay? All you have to say is okay?"

Jarrett gave him a blank stare. "I don't disagree with you. If you want to hit me again, get on with it. If not, can you please tell me where Anya is? She may not want to see me, but I need to see for myself that she is okay."

"Jeezus, Campbell. I really don't want to like you."

Jarrett offered a weak smile. "It's okay. Neither do I."

Luca just shook his head, confusion knitting his brow. "Anya's in the basement, second level down. It used to be a parking structure, so you'll have to take the stairs to the main floor, and then go down the hall to the lower level staircase. Our isolation rooms are down there. The attendant on the floor can direct you to the room."

Two
Jarrett

*J*ARRETT FOUND THE FLOOR LUCA HAD INDICATED quite easily, and the attendant led him back to a room with a heavy wood door. "You can go ahead and knock. She's still asleep."

Jarrett did as he was told. The door swung open to reveal a large, dark room filled with Anya's entire family, including Sam. They sat on soft chairs and sofas. Farrah was asleep on a cot in the far corner. Jarrett didn't see Fiona or Anya at first, but then he realized there was another room off to the side. The door was open, and he could see Anya asleep under a thin blanket. Ian stood leaning against a wall, his hand on Fiona's shoulder as she sat next to Anya's bed.

Pinky looked up. "Jarrett, I'm glad you're finally

awake. Please, come in."

Silently, he did as he was told, pulling the door shut behind him. The sitting room was dimly lit with crystal lamps, but the room where Anya slept was in full dark.

River saw him glance at it and said, "We'll have to shut the door between her room and the sitting room and limit visitors to one at a time when she starts to wake, but for now, it makes it easier for us to be close to her."

Jarrett nodded, finally understanding what the healers had meant when they'd said isolation room. The walls and floors were covered with thick coverings. He suspected there were sound-deafening spells on both rooms. When the doors were shut, the room she slept in would be pitch dark and the dimly lit sitting room would allow visitors in and out without exposing the occupant inside to the light and noise of the hall.

There had been no such rooms when he'd been changed. Unbidden, the memory of waking up and suddenly having all of his senses working in overdrive came back to him. Every tiny sound had been excruciatingly loud. Even candlelight had hurt his eyes. His senses had been so overwhelmed that it had taken him days just to be able to stand up.

These rooms would make Anya's transition a tiny bit bearable. For that, he was thankful.

"She's going to be okay? The virus...?" He trailed off.

River, the family member with medical training, answered. "Yes, the virus took hold. All of her injuries—the cut and her broken bones—healed normally. Now we are just waiting for the virus to do its thing. It's normal for her to sleep during the process, but Luca gave her a sedative as well, just in case."

"Okay, good. I..." He turned and looked at Pinky. "I'm sorry; I didn't have any other choice."

He saw from the expression in the other man's eyes that he didn't have to explain. "You did have a choice. And you made the correct one."

"She may not see it that way," Jarrett said.

Pinky nodded. "She may not, at first. You and I both know how hard the next weeks and months will be for her. But we made it through, and surrounded by less supportive people, I dare say. We got through it. And there is no doubt in my mind that Anya is ten times a stronger person than the two of us wrapped together."

Jarrett couldn't help but grin. "That she is. Speaking of strong," he said, nodding in Farrah's direction. "Is she going to be okay?"

Pinky nodded. "Physically, yes. Thanks for making sure she got cared for right away."

"What do you mean, physically?" Jarrett asked, concern for the young girl stabbing him in the gut. If it hadn't been for her, he'd never have been able to save Anya. Despite being drugged, she'd made her way from where she and Anya had been attacked to the docks where his boat was moored. She'd ignored her own suffering to make sure he got the scry-crystal the kidnappers had given her.

It was River who answered. "She's been through a lot. The drug they gave her paralyzed her, but it kept her fully conscious. She watched as they dragged Anya away, unable to do anything. Then she lay in that alley for nearly another hour waiting for the drug to wear off, frightened and vulnerable. On top of that, this is the second time she has been attacked in a year."

"You are afraid she will have some sort of lasting emotional trauma?" Jarrett asked.

River nodded. "She's sedated because she is hysterical every time she wakes up. We are keeping her in here so that if she does wake up, she's not alone."

Pinky walked over and stroked the sleeping girl's blonde hair. "She needs family around right now as much as Anya does."

"She's going to need that for a very long time. She'll need counseling with a psych-mage, as well as periodic energy testing. All of which Ian and I will make sure is paid for, since her parents are too sorry to even visit her," Fiona added, pure venom dripping from the last few words.

Jarrett understood her anger. He'd never met the Purcells, but he'd read the transcript of the interview Fiona and Ian had conducted with them when Farrah had been abducted last year. Anya had told him they hadn't visited Farrah in the hospital after that ordeal either, and they had refused Pinky's numerous invitations to dinner once she'd moved into the pub.

"I understand counseling, but why energy testing?" he asked, trying to get a grasp on the girl's condition.

"The ordeal with Bokor last year caused some major fluctuations and changes in her magic," Ian said. "Before she was kidnapped, she tested just above level-two mage status with telekinesis as her main power."

"I think she held back when she was tested," Fiona said in a tone that told Jarrett she'd had this conversation with Ian before.

"I agree. Her parents acted like being able to do magic was a disease, so I'm sure she tried to minimize what she could do," Ian said, patting her shoulder. "But she wouldn't have been able to hide much, and she tested at level seven three months ago. I'm also not sure that what Bokor did to her didn't change her powers some."

Pinky went back to sit next to River. "I've been working with her so she can learn to control her telekinesis, but she is scared of how strong she is. And I agree, I think there is something else happening with her abilities, but she won't try to use them in any other way or talk about anything she might be feeling."

River chimed in. "And that was when she was starting to feel safe and secure. This new trauma is likely to affect her control. Plus, we have no idea what long-lasting effects the drug might have."

Guilt knotted Jarrett's gut. This was all his fault. Anya had nearly been killed, and she had been sentenced to a long, lonely life she hadn't asked for. Farrah had gone through her second traumatic ordeal in six months, and who knew how it would affect the poor girl. And all because Cora had been trying to get even with him for killing the scumbag slave trader she'd fallen in love with.

He forced down the bile and anger that clogged his throat.

He walked into the dark room and stood next to the bed where Anya lay so still and quiet. "May I?" he asked.

Fiona moved, giving him her chair. He took Anya's hand in his and sat there for a long time, feeling the warm life pulsing through her. He'd sentenced her, without choice, to a life she hadn't chosen. It was something he'd sworn he'd never do to anyone. But he had. And though he had a world of guilt on his shoulders for her being in that situation, he couldn't bring himself to be sorry. He looked around the room and knew that no matter what, Anya would be okay. She had a loving family, and she would always have Pinky.

After a long moment, he looked at Sam. "Cora?"

"Nothing. Once Cora dropped Anya, the balloon went high fast. And with the wind blowing like it was, it was over the wall in seconds. My archers did their best, but other than landing several in the bottom of the basket, there wasn't much they could do. It was moving too quickly to track."

"I don't understand one thing. Do you think she was playing with us?" Jarrett asked.

"I can't be sure," Sam said.

"What do you mean by playing with us?" Fiona asked, an edge to her voice.

"Cora is a vampire. A very old one. She knows exactly where the arteries on the neck are, and how deep under the skin. It's as if she intentionally missed the artery. Otherwise, Anya..." Sam let his voice trail off.

"Would have been dead before she hit the ground," Fiona finished for him. "No, Cora wasn't playing. She is just a nutso crazy bitch, and she got too wrapped up to think a couple of things through. The blade wasn't quite as sharp as she probably thought it was. We found it; it had some micro-nicks in the edge. Sharp, but not enough. Also, the bitch defeated herself."

"What do you mean?"

"Anya had so much vampire venom in her system

that her heart had slowed to almost nothing. It saved her life," Fiona said, letting out a humorless laugh.

"She had bite marks?"

River looked at him strangely. "Yes, on her arm. That's how they knew the saliva was what saved her."

But Fiona knew what he was asking and answered his real question. "Like River said, there was a bite mark. One. It doesn't seem like enough to have slowed her heart so drastically, but the virus made it impossible to test her blood. Anything that was going on in there was cleaned out by the time we got her to the hospital."

Sam picked up where Fiona left off. "There's no visible connection between the new drug in town and Cora. I know you want there to be, but I think running into Python was just bad luck."

Jarrett snorted. Yeah, bad luck that he'd kicked into overdrive by alerting the man and Cora to his presence in Nash. If he hadn't done that, Anya wouldn't be lying in that bed right now.

He pulled her hand up to his lips, dropped a kiss on her palm, and then laid the hand gently on the bed. Now that he'd checked on her and knew for certain she would survive, it was time to do what came next.

"Fiona, can I talk to you outside, please?" Jarrett said. He looked at Sam, Ian, and Pinky. "The three of you should come as well; we'll need witnesses."

"For what?" Fiona asked.

"Just come, please," he said, not willing to do what needed to be done in the hospital ward where Anya laid suffering.

"River, will you be okay?" Fiona asked her youngest sister.

River looked up from where she was wiping Anya's forehead with a cool cloth. "It's fine. Luca said she wouldn't wake up for another six to eight hours. I'll stay here with her and Farrah."

"Okay," Pinky said, pressing his lips to River's forehead. "We'll be back in a few minutes."

Jarrett turned and strode out of the hospital, the other four trailing behind. He didn't stop until he came to a small garden area he remembered from a previous visit to the hospital years ago. It was obviously for patients and family to come enjoy fresh air, but it was empty at the moment.

He stopped in the center of the garden. Fiona crossed to him, the three men hanging back, watching intently.

"Jarrett, what's going on? You're kind of scaring me," she asked.

Wordlessly, Jarrett unsheathed his dagger and held it out to Fiona.

She stared at it. "Why are you giving me that?"

"Just take it," he said.

Confusion etched her features as she did as he

commanded. "Okay, now what?"

He pulled the hospital tunic off to reveal his chest. "Put it in my heart."

Ian took a step forward, but Fiona held her hand up to stop him. Fury replaced the confusion in her expression as she turned to the side and threw the knife down so hard it sank into the ground to the hilt. "Have you lost your fucking mind?" she asked more quietly than he expected.

"You said if I hurt her, you would put a knife in my heart. I'm just making it easy for you," he said, his words thick with pain.

"No, I said if she came to me with good reason and asked me to, then I would. At this point, she hasn't asked for anything. Even if she had, there isn't good reason. You just saved her life."

She didn't raise her voice. The calm steadiness of her words hit Jarrett's heart like tiny darts. He knew it was a sign of how upset she really was. Fiona had no problem raging in anger; it was when she got quiet that hell tended to break loose. He knew she was furious with him—hated him. And he deserved it. He didn't know why she wouldn't just go ahead and finish him.

"After first putting her in danger," he said.

Fiona's eyes went wide. "Really? You are taking responsibility for that psycho bitch's actions? I don't think so. You know, Jarrett, I am really pissed right now. And

I want to kill someone, but that person isn't you."

"It should be."

She rolled her eyes at him. "No, it shouldn't. But if you don't shut the fuck up and quit pissing me off, I'm going to kick your ass."

He put his hands behind his back, lacing his fingers together and leaving his body wide open to her. "Then do it," he ground out.

Fiona pulled her arm back and slammed her hand, open palmed, into the center of his chest. "I'm trying to be fucking sensitive here." She punctuated every few words with another hard push in the center of his chest, her voice rising as she spoke. "I know you're hurting, and I know it's because you care about Anya and seeing her hurt is ripping you apart. But I really can't take your fucking martyrdom right now. I nearly lost a sister tonight; I don't need to lose a brother on top of it."

She ended her tirade with a closed fist punch. To Jarrett's surprise, she burst into tears and threw herself at him, wrapping her arms around his waist.

At a loss, Jarrett wrapped his arms around her and rubbed her back, trying to soothe her sobs. Desperate for help, he looked over his head at Ian and Sam, who had remained silent throughout the exchange. Both men just shook their heads and held their hands up in a *don't-put-me-in-this* motion. He turned his gaze to

Pinky, who mirrored the other men's gesture.

"Don't look at me, son," he said, a sad smile playing across his tearstained face. "You saved my baby girl tonight. In my book, that makes you as much family as any one of my girls. We don't go around killing family. But if you try another stunt like that with the knife again, I might just help Fiona kick your ass."

With the other vampire's words, hot tears began streaming down his face as Jarrett cried for the first time in more than five hundred years. Suddenly, his entire body started shaking and he was too weak to stand. His knees buckled, and he and Fiona slid to the ground. They stayed like that, holding each other and sobbing for a long time as the other three men stood in front of them, shoulder to shoulder, blocking them from the prying eyes of passersby.

THREE
Anya

*R*AZOR BLADES SLICED MY SKIN. RED-HOT NEEDLES shot through my brain. Pain ripped at every part of my body—my head, my muscles, and my skin. I could even feel my toenails, and they hurt. As I tried to shift my body to relieve some of the misery, shards of fire shot through me. I thought I moaned, but the sound I heard couldn't have been me. It was so loud it set off a pulse of banging pain in my head. I tried to cover my ears, but my arms wouldn't move. The deafening moan sounded again, and then turned into an ear-splitting whimper.

"Shh." Another voice sounded. It was loud, yet oddly soothing.

"Hush, sweetheart. It's going to be okay," the voice

cooed, and I realized the speaker was River.

I tried to open my eyes, but my eyelids wouldn't work. It hurt to even try. Another whining groan sounded, and I realized I was the one making those irritating noises.

"Shh. It's okay. This will help you rest."

Something hard pressed painfully against my bottom lip. Warm, thick, and delicious liquid with a touch of bitter poured down the back of my throat. I swallowed, with no real idea how I'd pulled it off.

It seemed like an eternity passed, but then delicious warmth spread through me, pushing out the pain. I gave myself over to the sensation and let the warm blackness take me.

As the fog in my brain lifted and I climbed towards consciousness, it was as if I could feel every cell in my body, and they were all throbbing. There wasn't any real pain; it was more like every nerve ending in my body was on high alert. I tried lifting my eyelids and was surprised to find they were working properly. The room was dim, yet I could see everything clearly—not that there was much to see other than a darkly painted ceiling. When I turned my head, a sharp pain stabbed through my brain.

"Ouch," I said, my voice coming out in a loud croak.

"You're awake," a familiar voice said. Pinky's face hovered over mine. "Welcome back, darling girl."

His voice was breathy as if he were whispering, yet it was so loud I couldn't help but wince. Pain and worry etched his face, and he looked tired in a way I'd never seen before.

"What happened? Where am I?" My voice sounded dry, cracked, and a little panicky. I couldn't help it. Fear was starting to bubble up inside my stomach, churning it. I felt so odd. So much of my body hurt, and then there was the pain that wasn't pain, but more of an odd sensation. Where was I and why was Pinky staring down at me as if I'd just come back from the dead?

"Shh, it's okay," Pinky said, trying to soothe me.

He laid his hand on my arm, but it hurt and I flinched away. "Ouch," I said, tears filling my voice. "Pinky, what's going on? Why does it hurt?"

"Shh, don't talk. I need to get you some tea to soothe your throat. Lie there and rest."

Too weak to argue, I did as he bade, closing my eyes as I waited. I didn't drift back off to sleep, though. I was painfully aware of Pinky moving around the room. It was as if every sound was amplified, and every shift in the air blew across my skin. From the sounds, I'd guessed there was a teapot and crystal warming plate in the room. The scent of herbs and something else I couldn't name burst into the room as he slid the lids off glass containers. The odor grew stronger before softening as he combined them and poured hot water over the mixture.

Within a few minutes, Pinky was back by my side, though he had never actually left the room.

"Are you ready to try to sit up?" he asked, placing a mug on a table near my head.

"I think so," I said, opening my eyes and gazing up at his concerned face. I wasn't completely sure I was telling the truth, but curiosity was gnawing at me. I wanted to know what had happened, but I knew Pinky wouldn't tell me anything unless he thought I was doing better. Though better than what, I had no idea.

Several minutes later, I was cursing my curiosity and wishing I'd just told Pinky I wasn't ready to sit up yet. But I hadn't, and I was sitting up. If you could call propped against six pillows that forced me into a sitting position 'sitting up'. I wasn't even sure propped was the correct word because the moment Pinky let go of me after putting the last pillow into place, I'd collapsed back onto them, heaving from the pain and effort of getting into the position. Even with Pinky's help, it had been excruciating and exhausting.

"Here, this will help," Pinky said, holding the mug of warm liquid to my lips.

I sipped it, the strong flavor exploding in my mouth.

"What is that?" I asked after swallowing several mouthfuls.

"An herbal tea from River's garden. Chamomile, I think. There's some medicine to help your pain mixed in," he answered, setting the empty mug down. "Are you feeling any better?"

The medicine must be why it tasted so strong, but I was feeling a little better. "My throat doesn't hurt as much."

He smiled. "Good."

"Pinky, what happened? How did I get sick? What's wrong with me?" As I asked the questions, I watched my father's face grow serious, dread filling his eyes.

"I'm not sure right now is the best time. I think you need more rest."

"No," I said. It took every bit of energy I had, but I pushed his hand away as he tried to pull the blanket up around me. "I don't want to rest. Please, what happened? Why does everything hurt? Why are you the one taking care of me? Where's River and Fiona?"

With every question, my voice got more and more shrill. As I asked about my sisters, I realized just how strange, how wrong, it was for them not to be in the room. Were they sick too? Had something happened to them?

"Shh, Anya, calm down, baby. Fiona and River are okay," Pinky crooned as he gripped my hands between his. I realized I had been screaming out the thoughts in my head and that I was sobbing. "If you'll drink another mug of tea, I'll tell you, okay?"

I nodded, the motion making my head ache. "Okay," I said, trying to stop crying now that I realized I was doing it.

Pinky prepared another mug of tea, and we sat in silence as I drank it. The drink soothed me, sending a warming calm throughout my body. I suspected Pinky had put some sort of sedative in it that would knock me out soon, but I wasn't about to be deterred.

I held the mug out. "It's all gone. Now tell me what's wrong with me. I don't want to wake up again feeling so confused and scared."

The moment I spoke the words, I could see the determination to keep me in the dark fade from Pinky's demeanor. "Okay. I suppose knowing will be better than the fear of not knowing. What do you remember?"

I shook my head, grateful that the last cup of tea had taken away the stabbing pain behind my eyes. "I don't know. What do you mean?"

"Before you woke up here, what is the very last thing you remember doing?"

I thought hard, trying to focus. An image of Farrah and River formed in my mind. They were laughing. "I was at the market with Farrah and River. We were having lunch."

"You don't remember anything else? Do you know what you did after you left the market?"

I tried to think. I remembered telling River goodbye and walking towards the bridge with Farrah, but as we neared the bridge, everything got fuzzy, and then it was black. I couldn't remember. As I concentrated, another sharp throbbing started behind my left eye. I rubbed at my temple.

"I don't know, Pinky. I can't remember." My voice was nearing hysteria.

"Shh, it's okay," Pinky said, sitting on the edge of the bed and pulling me into his arms. "I'm going to tell you what happened, but I need you to promise to try to stay calm. You are safe and loved, and no matter what, you will be okay. Promise to remember that?"

I nestled my head against his chest, much as I did when I was a child. The comfort of his arms was accompanied by the feeling of dozens of tiny bees stinging my skin at every point where we touched, but I ignored it. A sense of dread was slipping over me, but I needed to know. "I promise."

As my adoptive father cradled me in his arms and rocked me like a baby, my entire world was pulled out from under my feet. He told me Farrah and I had been attacked, and that Farrah was fine, but I'd been kidnapped. He didn't have any other details except that Jarrett and Fiona tried to get me back, but the kidnapper, some woman named Cora, had cut my throat. I'd been dying and the only chance they'd had to save me was to infect me with the N-V virus.

The only way to save my life had been to change it forever. To change me forever. I was now a vampire.

As I tried to comprehend what Pinky was telling me, gray fog started blurring my thoughts. The sedative in the tea was starting to work. But I didn't want to go to sleep, not yet. I had to think. I was a vampire. Jarrett had saved my life. Jarrett—beautiful, sexy Jarrett—had saved me by changing me. Fear and confusion washed over me, but I was suddenly too tired and too weak to care about any of it.

Letting my mind drift away, I left behind my aches and pains. I let my thoughts be overtaken with Jarrett as I reminisced about what it felt like to be in his arms, whispering his name as sleep overtook me again.

Four
Anya

The next time I woke, I felt stronger. I still needed Pinky's help to sit up, but I didn't feel like I'd ran thirty miles after being trampled by a herd of oxen. That felt like progress.

I stared down at the mug of tea in my hands. "This isn't going to put me to sleep again, is it? I want to talk and see people."

Pinky flashed me one of his killer grins. "No worries. I didn't drug the tea."

I knew Pinky wouldn't lie to me, so I took a drink. The warm liquid flowed down my throat, soothing away the last of the leftover dryness and ache. As I took a second sip of the delicious tea, I suddenly realized what the not-chamomile flavor was.

I gazed at Pinky over the lip of the mug. "But you did put blood in it, didn't you?"

He nodded, his grin not wavering. "You need it to heal and get stronger. Putting it in tea or other liquids helps you get used to the flavor and your need to consume it. I used goat. It's my favorite."

I took another small sip, waiting for my gag reflex to kick in, but it didn't. The tea actually tasted good. My brain acknowledged the ick factor of drinking raw blood, but my body didn't seem to have the same problem. But what would the texture and taste of the blood be like straight up? My stomach quivered at the thought.

"Okay, but let's keep mixing it for a while. This could take some getting used to. Now, about seeing people."

Pinky shook his head. "Not until you've been looked over by a med-mage."

He went to the door and opened it slightly, flooding the room with light bright enough to hurt my eyes. "Go get Luca," he said to someone I couldn't see before shutting the door.

"Why do I have to be examined?" I whined. "I know I'm weak, but won't I get stronger with more blood? Just put more blood in my next cup. I'll be fine in a few hours." I'd seen Pinky get hurt before and he always healed quickly, even faster if he drank blood during the healing process.

"Sorry, but it doesn't work that way. At least, not yet," he said, sitting in the chair next to my bed. "The changing process is long and painful. The med-mages monitor your progress so that your senses aren't overloaded with too much stimuli at once. Trust me when I tell you, you don't want that."

The pained look that flitted across his features stabbed at me. "I guess you didn't have the benefit of such med-mages when you were changed?"

"No, though my experience wasn't as bad as it could have been. It was just very different back then. So much has changed since paranorms stepped out of the shadows after the Cataclysm. Even when I was changed, there were laws and guidelines set down by the Paranorm Council, but it was much harder to put them into practice. If you walked into a hospital claiming to be a vampire needing a med-mage, you would have been tossed into a padded cell. Though I suppose that would have helped a little."

I tried to laugh, but it came out a cackle. My throat wasn't as healed as I thought. "It probably wouldn't have been sound and light proof though," I said through a cough. It hadn't escaped my notice that even though I could see as well as if daylight were streaming in a window, there were no windows and none of the crystal lanterns in the room were lit. I also couldn't hear anything other than the slide of Pinky's clothes against the chair when he shifted.

Pinky refilled my cup. I was sipping on it when the door opened and Luca walked in. "Hey there, baby girl," he said, flashing his flirtiest smile.

Despite everything that had happened, despite the aches that still plagued me, I felt myself smile. Luca could always make me smile, even on the crummiest days. "I'm glad you're here. You can tell Pinky to let me see Jarrett and my sisters."

Luca's laugh was rich and throaty. "I see you've recovered your sass already. That's a step in the right direction. Let me take a look at you, and then we'll see about visitors."

I stuck my tongue out at him. "Fine."

Pinky laughed softly. "It's good to see you've decided to deal with all of this with maturity." He stood and dropped a kiss on my cheek. "I'm going to give you some privacy. I love you."

"Love you too," I said.

Once Pinky was gone, Luca sat down in the chair next to my bed. "How are you feeling, sweetness? And tell the truth."

I grimaced. "Truth? I feel like I went a hundred rounds with a juiced-up asshole and lost."

"Sounds just about right for this stage," he said, his honey-brown eyes twinkling with humor. "This is going to pull a little, but it won't hurt."

He reached his hand out. I felt something pull away from the skin at my throat, and then I saw a bandage in his hand.

My hand flew up to neck. "What the hell?"

"The bandage was spelled so you wouldn't feel it. We didn't want you to rip it off." He pulled my hand away so he could peer at my neck.

A strange coldness washed over me. Pinky had told me my throat had been cut, but it hadn't really registered. I would have a gash all the way across my throat. I winced. "Is it bad? Is it healing okay?" I asked, not sure I wanted to hear the answer.

Luca nodded. "It's fine. It is completely healed. The bandage was just to keep in a scar-reducing ointment."

I sighed with relief. "Oh, okay. How bad is the scar?"

He reached into a pocket and pulled out a small mirror. "See for yourself."

I peered at my reflection and gasped. My hair was knotted and sticking up all over my head. My naturally pale skin was sallow and dark purple ringed my eyes. The overall effect was terrifying. "I look hideous."

Luca shook his head. "You look ravishing, as always."

I ignored him and slid the mirror down so I could see my neck, bracing for the worst. But what I saw wasn't bad at all. There was a thin, pink line tracing under my chin from ear to ear like a bizarre smile, but that was all. I reached my hand up and traced the line with one fingertip. It was weird looking, but it wasn't the raised ugliness I had expected.

"You were lucky. Jarrett applied his blood directly to the wound, so the skin mended even before the virus took hold. There was a raised scar, but the magic-infused ointment broke it down. Eventually, it will fade the whole mark, and your skin will be flawless again," Luca said, taking the mirror from me.

I gave him a shaky smile. "Thanks."

Seeing the remnants of the scar really shoved home the fact I'd nearly died. Suddenly, my chest felt tight, like someone had sucker punched me in the center of my breastbone. A roaring throb started in my ears as I gasped for air. I squeezed my eyes shut, trying to shut out the pounding in my head.

Luca took my hand in one of his and used his other to grasp my chin and turn my face. "Anya, are you okay? Take a deep breath."

"I...I... can't." My voice was shrill and ragged.

"Yes, you can." Luca's voice was firm, yet patient. "Open your eyes, baby girl, and look at me."

I obeyed.

"You're having a panic attack. Look at me. Concentrate on my voice and just breathe. In. Out. In. Out."

As I peered into his burnt-honey eyes, I let the

smooth velvet of his voice wash over me, and I breathed in rhythm with his chant. Slowly, the tightness in my chest loosened and the roaring in my ears faded.

"That's it. Keep breathing. You're safe, and everything is going to be okay."

After several long moments, I began to feel normal again. Well, as normal as I'd felt since waking up as a vampire. "I don't know what just happened," I said.

"It's perfectly normal. You went through a major trauma, both mentally and physically. There will be lingering effects, which will be intensified by your body's changes. I don't want you to overdo it today, but tomorrow, we'll start you on regular sessions with a psych-mage who will help you learn how to manage your anxiety. Now, I'm going to do a diagnostic scan, just to see how you are doing overall, okay?"

I nodded. "Sure."

Luca's examination consisted of him running his hands over my entire body, pausing occasionally to make notes in a notebook. While it was exactly the procedure he'd followed last week when I'd been hurt at Pete's, it felt different this time. More intimate, somehow. As his fingers slid over my bare midriff, I felt my pulse quicken and my breath go ragged. Nothing about what he was doing was sensual, yet my body was reacting as if his touch were a lover's caress. It was embarrassing and arousing at the same time.

Sensing my discomfort, Luca looked up at me and flashed me a wicked grin. "I'd like to take credit for what you are feeling right now, but I can't. Don't worry. Like the panic attack, this is perfectly normal. Your hormones are in overdrive. I'll make this as quick and pleasure-less as possible."

I laughed, but my humor was quickly replaced by more quivering sensations. It didn't help matters that the med-mage was deliciously sexy. I closed my eyes, but that was a colossal mistake. Jarrett's face immediately popped into my mind as Luca's hand slid across my thigh. I moaned.

Luca laughed.

My eyes flew open, and I gave a weird yip. "Sorry."

"Don't be." He gave me a mischievous wink. "Probably the best thing that has happened to me all day. And that shade of red is lovely on you."

I didn't have to ask what he meant; my face was burning with embarrassment. Instead, I stuck my tongue out at him. "Are you this professional with all of your patients?"

"Just the ones I adore, baby girl," he said with a laugh. He pulled the sheet back over me. "But I'm all done."

I let out a sigh of relief. "So what's the verdict? Can I have visitors?"

"Two more tests first. Close your eyes."

I did as he asked. A few seconds later, even behind my eyelids, I could tell a lamp had been activated.

"Okay, slowly open your eyes," Luca said.

I did as I was told, and bright light flooded my eyes. I felt like I was staring directly at the sun.

I couldn't see him, being temporarily blinded as I was, but I knew Luca stood right next to me. "I know it hurts, but give it a minute. Your eyes should start adjusting."

Within a few seconds, the light seemed to dim, and the spots in front of my eyes disappeared. I could see again, though the room was very brightly lit. But considering how my body had been acting, I wondered if it really was. "I'm guessing that lamp is on the lowest setting," I said, my voice dry.

"Yep. It will take time, but eventually, your eyes will get used to it and you will be able to tolerate more light. But this will make it possible for you to have visitors who aren't vampires."

My face split into a smile. That was well worth the forming headache.

Sitting in the chair next to me, Luca held out a towel. "We are going to test your strength now. Try to pull the towel out of my hand."

I gave him a dubious look. "Okay, but I'm going to be honest, I feel about as strong as a newborn kitten. I'm actually pretty disappointed. I thought vampires were super strong, but I have zero energy."

I grasped the towel and gave it a gentle tug. There was a loud ripping sound, and suddenly, the towel was in shreds.

My jaw dropped. I had no words. Luca, on the other hand, was full of them.

"I'd say your super strength is coming in quite nicely. I know you feel frail right now, and you are. At risk of repeating myself for the umpteenth time, your body is going through constant changes right now. Though you have physical strength, doing too much right now could cause damage. Eventually, we'll start working on teaching you how to adjust to that strength, but for now, I don't want you doing anything but lying in that bed. I mean it. Even when going to the bathroom, a healer or attendant is to carry you. Your family can visit for short periods, one at a time. But I want you resting as much as possible."

In truth, I was already too tired to argue. "Okay. I promise to do nothing but lay here. Can I see Jarrett and my family now?"

He stood, smiling down at me. "I think Sam had Campbell tied up with some Blade business, but I'll scry over and let them know you are ready for visitors. I'll send your sisters in first. I'll see you tomorrow, baby girl." He dropped a kiss on my forehead and left.

River was the first to visit. With the assistance of

a healer, she helped me get cleaned up. Brushing my hair was a tedious, tear-inducing affair, and I had her braid it to keep it from knotting up again. Then, once I was all clean, Farrah came in. She only stayed a moment before hastily retreating. While helping me clean up, River explained that Farrah had been nearly inconsolable since "the incident". That was what we were calling my abduction now. I felt bad for Farrah, but I didn't know how to help her. Not yet, at least. Maybe once I was up and around and she could see that I was okay, she'd feel less guilty. Though she had nothing to feel guilty about.

Finally, Fiona came in. The moment she walked in, I could see the guilt etched into her face. But I knew how to deal with her.

"If you even think of apologizing to me for helping save my life, the moment I'm able, I'll slap you. And I have vampire strength now, so it'll hurt. A lot."

She burst into a mixture of laugh-tears and that was that. We sat and talked a lot about nothing. It was lovely to not think about anything but random everyday stuff, but very quickly, I felt my eyes starting to droop. This time, it was without the aid of drugged tea.

"Why don't you get some rest? I'll stay here," Fiona said.

"I was hoping to see Jarrett," I protested. I was starting to get a little anxious about the fact he hadn't shown up yet. Was whatever Sam had him doing for the Blades that important? Or did he just not want to see me?

"You might as well get some rest. It will be a couple of more hours before we will be able to get tribunal approval for him to visit," Fiona said.

Tribunal approval? That made no sense. "I don't understand. Why would he need permission?"

Fiona's eyes narrowed. "Neither Pinky nor Luca told you?"

I could feel my chest start to tighten again, and I forced myself to take slow, deep breaths. "Tell me what?"

"Jarrett was arrested."

FIVE
Jarrett

*The walls were closing in on him. The eight-*by-eight room was more than adequate for its normal use. There was just enough space for a desk, narrow bed, and a tall cabinet that held spare clothes and weapons.

In fact, considering how little he used his room in the Nash Blades Headquarters, he'd always thought it was too big. It was even more spacious than his cabin on The Minnow. But he never spent much time in his cabin, either. Except the past couple of weeks. He'd spent plenty of time in his cabin with Anya.

"Ugh." With an audible grunt, he popped off the narrow bed and began pacing the space between the back wall and the door again. After a little over sixty hours in here, he'd worn a hole in the already threadbare carpet.

It could be worse, he knew. Instead of being allowed to spend his pre-tribunal confinement in the comfort of his own room—after the weapons cabinet had been cleared, of course—he could have been stuck in an even smaller eight-by-four cell that held a narrow cot and a bucket for "necessities". This room was the height of luxury compared to that, and the guard at the door escorted him down the hall to the restroom as needed.

It wasn't just the confined space that was bothering him. It was that, combined with being alone and inactive. Although the nature of his job, being a spy and assassin, meant he was alone most of the time, it had never bothered him before. But he'd always been busy, had his mind occupied with a case, or at the very least was on his boat or in the great outdoors. Cooped up in here, all he had to do was pace and think. It was the thinking that was driving him mad.

His thoughts were a jumble of Cora and Anya. The worry and guilt he'd felt only two weeks ago over Cora was gone, replaced with fury, hate, and another kind of guilt. He no longer felt remorseful that he hadn't saved her, hadn't stopped her from jumping off that rooftop in Detroit. No, now he was sorry he hadn't made sure she was dead, or ended her himself.

In the first few hours of his confinement, he'd mentally beat himself bloody with the thought that he should have seen just how much she'd changed that night. He should have seen how different she was as she'd shrieked about her love for a dead slave trader. But then, had she actually changed?

After really thinking about it, he realized Cora's eventual betrayal of the laws the Black Blade Guard swore to uphold had been inevitable. The fact that it had taken so many centuries only owed to the fact that she'd never found a way of life that had suited her better. Something the slave trader, Dread, had obviously offered her.

Jarrett, and many like him, had been changed in order to replenish the vampiric ranks at the end of long and bloody war known to norm history as The Spanish Inquisition. He had been sought out with the express purpose of being pressed into service of the Black Blade Guard. The Blades had been formed in the midst of the Inquisition, at the same time as the Paranorm Council of Elders.

But Cora was centuries older than he was. She had been changed during a brutal and bloody time. There had been no universal rule of law over the paranorm races—mage, vampire, and shifter. They did as they pleased, fought amongst themselves, and norms often got caught in the crossfire. The Inquisition started as a war between mages and vampires, but then it bloomed into the hunting and execution of all paranorms. The races were forced to band together, and the Paranorm Council of Elders was formed. The Black Blade Guard were their protectors and their army during the long and devastating war.

Jarrett didn't know exactly when or why Cora had joined the Blades, but he'd always suspected it had been when they first formed, perhaps so she could continue to fight in the war. Cora had decent fighting skills, but it was her blood lust that made her an excellent soldier, earning her several commendations from the Council of Elders. She'd told him she'd stayed on as a Blade because it was one of the few jobs where being a woman didn't hold her back. She told him couldn't see herself going back to being a barmaid for eternity, though she'd had to play one often enough when she was undercover.

Jarrett had always had a tiny, wormy suspicion that Cora had stayed with the Blades, and joined the Kukri division, because she enjoyed the violence and carnage a little too much. As an agent, especially in those early centuries, she was outside the paranorm laws. Blades too often broke the laws in order to enforce them. Whereas he had joined the Kukri for the challenge and because he wanted to keep the world safe, he had always thought Cora had become an assassin because she enjoyed killing. Now he was sure of it.

Cora wasn't a nice person. He'd known that. But in his naiveté, and perhaps because he'd been blinded by their complicated personal history, he'd thought she was honorable deep down. He'd believed, so strongly, that her reaction to Dread's death had been the result of brainwashing. He'd hoped that if he could find her, he could help her through it and back to the good person she was. Only there was no good in Cora. She was, had always been, rotten to her very core.

Tough, sweet, incredible Anya had reaped the consequences of his ignorance, of his stupidity. She hadn't asked for any of this. She had been brutalized and had her life turned upside down all because he'd refused to see the truth. That was the guilt he now bore.

Fiona had been allowed to visit him several times and kept him updated on Anya's condition. She'd finally awoken and was doing okay, but she wasn't allowed visitors yet. The relief he'd felt upon hearing that news had been immeasurable.

It was rare, but some people died after being infected with N-V. Sometimes because they had been infected for the same reason as Anya, but the N-V hadn't been able to heal their injuries quickly enough. There were also those whose body rejected the N-V virus. Though no immunity had been found—or a vaccine would have been developed—there was a small group of people whose bodies had a negative reaction to N-V. This usually happened if the person had unknown shifter ancestry.

Despite not knowing much about her ancestry, the risk had been worth it. She was alive. And she would stay alive, perhaps forever.

That was where his elation ended. He knew that what he'd done to her had been both a blessing and a curse. It was very likely that she would not thank him for choosing a long, lonely life for her. But if she let him, he would do whatever it took to make it up to her.

"I'm sorry, sir, but no one is allowed in." The voice of the guard posted outside his door pulled Jarrett out of his musings.

"I'm the healer in charge of Agent Campbell's recovery. I'm here for his post-transfusion checkup," a familiar voice replied.

Jarrett let out an audible groan and dropped onto his bed, propping his back up against a wall.

"Are you here to here to hit me again, Jensen? Because I know I was given a clean bill of health with no further checkups ordered," he said as Luca shut the door.

"As tempting as that is, no." Luca flashed a grin, pulling the desk chair out and settling down. "I thought you might want to know that I just cleared Anya for brief visits, one person at a time. I let Sam know, and he's processing the visitation request. Apparently, everything in your case has to go directly through the High Tribunal."

Though the last wasn't formed as a question, Jarrett could hear the curiosity in the med-mage's voice. It made sense. Though Luca was technically employed by the Blades, he wasn't an agent. The hierarchy of command and legal proceedings would be unfamiliar.

"When a paranorm is arrested under normal circumstances, the local Blade Commander, in this case, Sam, has complete jurisdiction over where and how the subject is held up until his trial. The tribunal determines guilt or innocence, type of punishment, and length of punishment. The commander, or rather the clerk he assigns to the duty, determines at what prison or work camp the convict will serve out his sentence, or what form of community service, or their execution date."

Luca nodded, his face showing genuine interest. "I see. So Sam has almost full authority. I can't see him having his hand in every criminal case that comes through."

Jarrett laughed. "Me either. Actually, there's a whole division of clerks who work out all of that, though Sam has been known to stick his two cents in for particular cases. But the gist of it is, he's the boss. What he says goes."

"But not this time?"

Jarrett shook his head and sat up straighter. "If a Blade agent is accused of a crime, the commander's jurisdiction becomes limited, or is even terminated, depending upon the rank of the accused. In my case, the High Tribunal is allowing Sam limited authority, thus my plus digs." He waved a hand around at his room. "But everything has to be cleared through them first. Especially something like leaving my "prison cell" and venturing out of the headquarters building. Even if it's just to go across the street. They haven't taken Sam's authority away completely because, technically, I'm not actually under his command and my crime was committed in his city."

"Saving a life is never a crime," Luca said, his tone full of conviction.

Jarrett smirked. He was starting to like this guy, and it annoyed him. "Unless you do it by using illegal means in a city-state with a couple of senators who proposed a law to ban even voluntary N-V infection."

"Those two are idiots. It amazes me that people never seem to learn from history. But they'll be gone at the next election," Luca said, shaking his head in disgust.

"Unfortunately, stupidity was one thing the Cataclysm couldn't eradicate," Jarret said with a snorting laugh, but then he sobered. "But you didn't come over here to talk politics. Nor did you come to tell me about Anya. You could have easily scryed Sam, and he would have told me, or sent someone to get me when the approval for visitation went through. So why are you really here?"

Straightening in his chair, Luca met Jarrett's eyes, his face serious. "I came to tell you to be careful with Anya."

Jarrett leaned back against the wall again, his arms across his chest. His casual position belied the tension that snapped his muscles taut the moment the other man said Anya's name. "Are you telling me this as her healer, her friend, or the guy who wants to sleep with her?"

Luca's jaw tightened, his teeth grinding together. "I guess a little bit of all three."

Jarrett respected the fact that the med-mage had acknowledged his attraction to Anya. While Jarrett did get the vibe that Luca would never push Anya for anything beyond friendship, it had been clear from the first time they'd met that the med-mage's feelings for Anya were anything but platonic. But she seemed completely oblivious, convinced that his flirtations were nothing more than friendly banter.

Even though his respect for the man was growing, Jarrett did not appreciate, want, or need Luca's opinion on his relationship with Anya. "Seems to me that your rights to give me input on how to treat Anya begin and end with your role as her doctor."

Luca stood, and for a moment, Jarrett thought the med-mage was going to start pacing the room as he had done just a little bit earlier. Instead, Luca pushed the chair back into place under the desk. "Fine. As her healer, I'm telling you to be gentle with her. Try not to upset her. I'm sure I don't need to tell you the kind of physical and emotional havoc her body is playing on her right now. Just don't upset her."

No, he didn't have to explain what Anya was going through right now. Jarrett knew all too well. It had been more than five hundred years since he'd gone through the change, but that was not something you ever forgot. Back then, there weren't isolation chambers or skilled med-mages at the ready to relieve the pain. Even with the Blade that had changed him and her commanding officer by his side, helping him, he had endured weeks of torture until his body had adjusted.

"I'll be careful with her," he said softly.

He turned to leave, but stopped with his hand on the doorknob. For a long moment, he stood there, but then he let go and turned back to Jarrett.

"Screw this. I don't care if you think I'm overstepping my bounds or not. I'm going to say what I came to say, and you're going to listen, even if I have to bring that guard in here to hold you down."

Jarrett didn't move, only smirked. "Hit me with your best shot, Doc."

"Anya is in love with you."

Luca's flatly delivered words hit Jarrett solidly in the solar plexus as sure as if they'd been a well-aimed fist.

"Wha...what makes you think that?" he asked, furious at how gruff he sounded. He just couldn't catch his breath.

Luca folded his arms across his chest and leaned against the door, one knee up. "You mean other than how she looks at you whenever you are anywhere near each other? It's like she wants to melt into you."

"Well, we do have a very satisfying sexual relationship. I can't help it if she's always turned on when we're together," Jarrett shot back, and then he grinned as the med-mage emitted a sound that was dangerously close to a snarl.

With visible effort to not throw a punch at Jarrett, Luca continued. "You were the first person she asked for. She wanted to see you even before her sisters. If you know her at all, then you understand how important her sisters are to her. Asking to see you first shows how important you have become to her. If she's not in love with you, she is as close to it as I've ever seen her."

Jarrett did understand. But he couldn't bring himself to let Luca see how much his words were affecting him. "I do know Anya. Probably better and in more ways than you do."

Luca's face went crimson. "You know what? You're an ass. I don't even know why I'm trying to help you. Actually, I'm not. I'm trying to help Anya avoid getting broken beyond repair."

"I have no intention of hurting Anya," Jarrett gritted out.

Luca let out an exasperated breath. "I believe you. But unintentional pain usually hurts the worst. I'm just saying, you have to spend the next year with her, living with her, being with her every single day. You need to figure out your intentions beyond that year and set ground rules from the start. Not just for you, but for her. I know she seems tough as nails, but she isn't. If you let her fall deeper in love with you and then leave her, it will destroy her."

SIX
Jarrett

T WAS SIX HOURS AND TWENTY-THREE MINUTES FROM the time Luca left Jarrett's room until Sam arrived to escort him to City Hospital to visit Anya. Jarrett knew that was the exact amount of time because he had counted every single minute as it passed.

He would have tracked the seconds, as well, but he had been too busy running Lucas' words over and over in his head. If the med-mage was correct, and Anya's feelings for Jarrett ran as deeply as Luca suspected, then perhaps she would be open to the plan Jarrett had concocted.

Before speaking to Luca, Jarrett had been determined to make up for his part in changing Anya's life, but he hadn't been certain how to go about it. But now he knew. He would make sure she was taken care of, and not just for the year he was legally obligated. If she let him, he would make sure she would never be alone in the world.

"Take your time. I'll hang out here with Fiona," Sam said, walking into the sitting room attached to Anya's room and settling down on the upholstered sofa next to Fiona.

"Yeah, go on in," Fiona said. "I let her know you were on your way so she's expecting you."

Jarrett took a deep breath and pushed the door open, staying behind it so she couldn't see him, but he couldn't see her either. He tapped lightly on the wood.

"Come in."

Her whispered voice washed over him like a healing balm. It wasn't until that moment, as his muscles loosened and unfurled, that he realized how tense he'd been since he'd awoken in his hospital room. No, since the moment he'd learned she'd been taken. There had been a two-ton elephant sitting on his chest since that moment and it wasn't until now, when it had stood up and loped off, that he'd even known it.

The wide grin that formed on his face didn't have to be faked or pasted. It came as naturally as breathing now. Just the sound of her voice told him she was okay, and a strange, light airiness filled him inside. He couldn't stop smiling if he tried.

He stuck his head around the edge of the door. "Hiya, Ginger."

The sight of her in the bed, her pale skin nearly as white as the sheets, dark purple circles around her eyes, nearly caused his smile to slip. But then she looked up at him, and her entire face lit up. Her smile was tired, but wide and genuine, and in her eyes, he recognized the same light that bubbled in the pit of his stomach. She was happy to see him.

"Jarrett! I'm so glad you came." Her voice was soft and raspy, but there was a strength behind it. She was going to be okay.

He walked on clouds as he crossed the room and settled in the chair situated right next to the bed. "Are you kidding? Miss seeing you forced to be still for more than two seconds at a time? Not a chance."

She stuck her tongue out at him. Yep, she was definitely okay.

"How are you feeling?" he asked.

"Good." She paused. "Okay, that's a lie. I feel like day-old crap on a cracker. But I'm feeling better than I was, and they say I'll keep improving. And eventually, the pounding in my head will go away for good and stop coming back."

"Whoever "they" are, they are right. You'll get used to the heightened senses. Light and sounds won't hurt anymore. Pretty soon you will wonder how you ever lived with your senses as dull as they used to be."

She laughed. "I know. It's just odd feeling so weak. I mean, vampires are supposed to be strong and heal fast. I want to be like that."

"We are, and you will be. It just takes time. Didn't the healer explain about how the N-V virus works? It changes every cell of your body. Yes, eventually, your body will work more efficiently, be stronger, heal fast, and be almost indestructible. But the changes take time and energy."

Her smile was sweet. "Yes, Luca explained it all to me. I'm just impatient. You know me."

He had no idea why, but those last three words made his stomach do strange, twisty things. *You know me.* He wasn't sure he did know her, not completely. But he did. He really did.

"You'll be back to your old, bad-ass self in no time. Just gotta be patient, even though I know that's a foreign concept to you," he said.

"I know. I'll be better than new. Thanks to you."

She gave him a bright, soul-shattering smile. That light, airy feeling grew, flowing through him like bubbles in his blood.

"So, you don't hate me?"

Her eyes widened. "Are you kidding me? You saved my life. You're my Super-guy."

For the first time in days, Jarret laughed. It was a deep, throaty belly laugh. "You mean Superman?" he asked when he could breathe again.

She rolled her eyes, her smile not wavering. "Whatever. Pinky tried explaining superheroes to me, but I couldn't remember them all."

"I'm impressed you even tried," he said, wondering if she would ever cease to amaze him.

Suddenly, her face sobered, her grin fading. "But I'm worried about you. Fiona said you were arrested. That's just not fair."

Agitation showed in her eyes and the way her hands started fidgeting. Remembering Luca's directive not to upset her, Jarrett took her hand in his, hoping to calm her.

"It's okay," he said, using extra effort to make his voice soothing. "It's really just a formality. The city-state takes the vampire laws seriously, and rightly so. The tribunal is just a reminder that there was a breach in protocol. They'll give me a verbal, or perhaps written, reprimand and put you in my care for a year, which is the law anyway."

She nodded her understanding. "The one-year custody requirement that requires you to teach me vampire law, control of my body and emotions, and makes you responsible for my actions."

"Though, because of the special circumstances,

they will probably offer you the choice of waiving my responsibility of you. But to do that, you would have to have another vampire willing to step in and be your guardian for a year."

"Like Pinky?"

Relief that her first thought was her adopted father and not Luca speared through him. He avoided smirking only through great effort. "Yes, Pinky would fit the requirements. If he was okay with it, and it was what you wanted, they would probably grant him guardianship."

Her eyes shifted, uncertain. "It's probably for the best, right?" she said with a nervous titter. "I mean, you are a Blade, a Kukri, even. You have a job and a life to get back to. You don't want to be stuck in Nash City for a year having to watch over me."

He took a deep, steadying breath. It was now or never. "No, I don't want to watch over you for a year."

Her face fell, her mouth quivering, but he continued. "I want to watch over you for always. Anya, will you marry me?"

SEVEN
Anya

MARRY ME. MARRY ME. MARRY ME.

I flattened my hand against the bed, hoping that contact with something solid and still would stop the world from shifting around me. Even in the dark, quiet room, there were so many new sensations flying at me I could barely think, and now those words were bouncing around inside my skull, making me dizzy.

Marry me. Marry me. Marry me.

I was rattled, overwhelmed, confused. I wanted to feel happy, elated, whatever you were supposed to feel at a moment like this. But something didn't feel right, and it wasn't because of the changes going on inside my body. He hadn't said he loved me. Wasn't some sort of profession of undying love supposed to go hand in hand with a marriage proposal?

"You..." I forgot to whisper and the sound of my voice boomed through my head, setting it to pounding again. Wincing, I lowered my voice to a breathy whisper and repeated, "You want to marry me?"

"It makes sense. I can quit the Blades, and we'll settle wherever you want. You won't have to be alone." I knew he was whispering, yet his voice still filled the room as if he were shouting.

More confusion wrapped around my blurry mind. "You want to marry me so I won't be alone? I don't understand."

He spoke slowly, as if to a small child—which I actually felt like at the moment. "Under law, I am responsible for you for the next year. But after that, you will be alone. You don't deserve that. You didn't ask for this life. I'm responsible for you being a vampire, and I'll take care of you. Not just for the year. For always. I'll quit the Blades, marry you, and take care of you. You won't have to be alone."

Responsible. He'd said the word twice, but not once did he use the word love. Realization seeped through the fog in my brain. Jarrett was proposing, but not because he loved me, or even cared about me. He had only asked me to marry him out of guilt.

As my brain cleared, understanding began to form.

Vampires were practically immortal. They spent centuries on earth watching as friends and loved ones died, decade after decade. That was one of the reasons why the laws governing the spreading of the N-V virus were so stringent in Nash. A person had to choose the life of a vampire, with full knowledge of the consequences. By saving my life, he'd taken that choice away, and now he felt guilty that I would someday have to watch my sisters die.

A rush of emotions burst over me in what felt like a physical wave of scalding water. They were so jumbled I couldn't sort them out. Anguish at the thought of losing my sisters—no matter how far in the future that might be, fear of not knowing what my life would be like now, hurt, sadness, and disappointment at the fact that Jarrett didn't love me, only pitied me. Then they were all washed away by white-hot fury.

My mind cleared, and everything assaulting my heightened senses dulled to white noise as I let the anger flow over me. I took it in, embraced it. No way in hell was I going to be anyone's pity project. Especially not Jarrett Campbell's.

The intensity of my emotions was unfamiliar, and it took me several moments before I felt I could speak without showing them. I tried to keep my voice steady, nonchalant, but was surprised when my words came out calm and cold. "You forget that I'm the daughter of a vampire; I won't be alone in the world. We had a good time together, but that is no foundation for getting married and spending eternity together. I don't want you to give up your career and marry me out of pity. I don't need you to."

When he opened his mouth to speak, I held up a hand, cutting off his words.

"You saved my life, and for that, I am grateful. You have no responsibilities beyond that. I know what the laws say, but I'm sure that with Fiona's connections, Pinky can retain guardianship over me for the next year. Now, as I'm sure you can understand, I'm feeling a bit overwhelmed by the world and would like to rest."

I eased my aching body over in the bed, giving him my back. For long moments, Jarrett's breaths echoed off the walls as I waited for him to take the hint. Finally, I heard his footsteps cross to the door.

As the door clicked, signaling his departure, the reality of my situation slammed into me with the force of a thousand punches. My body shrank in on itself, curling into the fetal position. I pressed my face into my pillow, my chest heaving as my heart ripped to shreds by a pain so intense it was almost physical.

Jarrett had wanted to marry me and tie himself to me for an eternity out of guilt. He felt guilty because one day, I'd be all alone. It had taken a moment for me to realize what that had really meant. Now that I did,

I wished away the knowledge with every fiber of my being.

With the exception of Pinky, I would outlive my entire family. Which meant one day, I would have to sit by, powerless, as my sisters died. How could I possibly stand that?

The tears started then, scalding hot as they welled up in my eyes before flooding down my face. My body shook uncontrollably as sobs rocked me, croaking up out of my throat in hoarse rasps. Pain clutched at me, and I no longer knew what was physical and what was emotional. It all balled together into a searing heat that clawed at my skin, throbbed in my head, and pulsed in my heart.

I felt sure I would die from it, and I welcomed the thought. If I died now, I would be spared watching my family die in the future. Even in my grief, I knew that was incredibly selfish. I'd just seen the joy on my sisters' faces as they'd sat with me, listened to the sorrow in their voices as they told me how scared they'd been to lose me. I knew if I died, it would hurt them. Especially Fiona, who had risked her career by assisting Jarrett. But they would eventually get on with their lives, lives that would be so short in comparison to what mine would be as a vampire.

Pinky would carry my loss with him, I knew. But he'd already gotten used to it. He had known from the moment he met us, he would someday lose us. He had the pub to keep him going and distract him. Part of me knew how ridiculous my thoughts were, but the rest of me didn't care. Soon, that rational part of me was covered in grief and self-pity, and I couldn't hear it in my thoughts any more.

A knock sounded on the door, and I groaned. I didn't want visitors. Not now, not ever. "Go away," I said, but my voice came out in a harsh rasp that even I barely heard.

"Hey, sweetness, just checking... Anya?" Luca was next to me in an instant, his strong hands rolling me over onto my back, his hands automatically starting to run over my body, checking for injury. "Anya, what's wrong? What hurts?"

"Everything," I said in barely more than a whisper. "I don't want to do this, Luca."

His hands stopped checking me and came up to cradle my tear-splotched face. "Do what, sweet girl?"

"This. Be a vampire. Watch my family die. I don't want to do it. I want to die." My words came out haltingly between sobs and gasps.

Wordlessly, Luca gathered me to him. His touch might have hurt on my skin. It blended with all the other pain, but I didn't even notice. I did feel the warmth of his arms around me, and it brought a small bit of comfort. I went limp against him as he rubbed my back and murmured comforting words I couldn't make out over my own sobs.

There was a sharp pain in my neck. Within seconds, the sharp edges on the agony in my body began to dull. Everything began to soften and blur, and my eyelids felt incredibly heavy. Just before I lowered them, Luca's hand moved across my line of site and I saw the syringe in his hand.

He hadn't relied on tea to drug me this time. Good, I wasn't thirsty. I was tired, and I just wanted everything to go away for a while. I sagged against the pillows, Luca's arms still around me. I felt him shift and stretch his body out next to mine.

"Go to sleep, baby girl," he whispered, his lips close to my ear. "Rest now."

I started to open my mouth to say something back to him, but I was just too exhausted. Instead, I closed my eyes and let myself sink into his warmth. It wasn't long before drug-induced sleep overtook me yet again.

A soft knock sounded at the door.

"Go away," I called out, but the door opened anyway. "How many times do I have to say I don't want to see anyone?"

"Too bad; they want to see you," Fiona said as she

came into the hospital room.

I sighed, exasperated. "I'm really not up to company right now."

"Yes, I know. Luca explained that you need time to come to grips with all that has happened," she said. Her tone held no sign of annoyance, yet it wasn't comforting either. "But you don't have any choice about this. The tribunal has called for the hearing to take place in an hour."

Ahh, yes. The hearing that would determine Fiona and Jarrett's punishment for saving my life. "Already?" I asked, not bothering to turn over to look at her. "It's only been a few hours since Luca cleared me for visitors."

"Thirty-six, actually. And they are impatient to get it over with. Luca tried stalling them. He said you were not ready to leave isolation yet. But they aren't willing to wait any longer. They are holding the hearing here in the hospital. That was the most compromise they would make."

I did not want to deal with this, so I pulled the blanket tighter around me. "I already gave my statement to the Blade agents this morning and absolved the two of you from wrongdoing. Isn't that enough?"

"You don't get it, do you? This is very serious." There was a harsh, annoyed edge to Fiona's words, even as she tried to keep her voice low.

I didn't bother telling her she didn't have to whisper. My tolerance to sounds had been building up. Normal tones, while still sounding louder than they used to, didn't hurt my head any more. The past few times they'd come in to do checkups, Luca and the nurse had been speaking normally.

"I know you could both lose your jobs. But I told them you did what you thought was the best solution. I told them I was glad you saved my life." Of course, I'd lied. But it was a little thing to keep Fiona and Jarrett out of trouble. I knew they really had done what they had thought was right, and they shouldn't be punished for it. Especially not Fiona, who had been facing the loss of a sister. "I also signed a waiver absolving Jarrett of responsibility for me. Pinky sat in on the interview and counter-signed, taking custody of me for the first year of my life as a vampire, as the law requires."

Fiona came around to stand in front of my face, but I didn't look up at her. She crouched down so that we were eye to eye. I had three choices—look at her while she spoke, close my eyes, or turn over. I wanted to be left alone, but I wasn't childish. I stared back at her, unblinking.

"Anya, those papers you signed this morning mean nothing. They are a formality under normal circumstances. But nothing about this situation is normal. Jarrett infected you with N-V without your permission within Nash City borders. Under "normal circumstances," he would have been executed before you were coherent enough to sign a waiver."

Alarmed at the ferocity behind her eyes, I sat up in the bed. "But you are a witness, so is Sam. You can testify that if he hadn't, I would have died. Jarrett's a Blade, a Kukri even. That should give him more authority to do what is necessary to save a life."

She nodded. "Those are the only reasons he's even getting a trial. You know as well as I do that the vampire laws are strictly enforced in all city-states allied under the Paranorm Council, especially in Nash."

"But the tribunal is just a formality; Jarrett said so. He said both of you would be cleared of any wrongdoing as long as I gave a statement," I said, but Fiona was starting to scare me.

Fiona shook her head, her lips pursed. "If it had taken place in the Outer Zones, there would have been no issue at all. But the senate and the Paranorm Council have numerous agreements in place about unlicensed N-V infection. The Nash city-state senate has contacted the Council of Elders and demanded a High Tribunal."

The words turned my blood to ice. Normal court sessions for paranorm criminals on trial by the Blades were tried by a tribunal of magistrates—one mage, one vampire, and one shifter. There were three sets of judges for the Nash City division who rotated cases, but there was one tribunal, the High Tribunal, that supervised them and were a direct link between the judges and the Paranorm Council of Elders.

While Sam had full autonomy to run the Nash City Black Blade Guards, the High Tribunal had jurisdiction over all legal proceedings. The High Tribunal did not, as a rule, conduct trials. The exception was crimes that the Council of Elders had taken an interest in or cases against Blade agents.

Before I could say anything, Fiona continued. "I will very likely lose my job today for my role as an accessory. And I'm okay with that. It's just a job, and Ian has already set up an interview for me at the academy for a position teaching hand-to-hand combat. Or I can always join the Mercenary's Guild."

I never thought Fiona would lose her job. "Surely, they won't fire you. You are my sister. Of course you did whatever it took to save my life, and you didn't even do anything."

"Which is why the only thing that will happen to me is losing my job. I knew the moment I told Jarrett to do whatever it took what I was risking. And he knew what he was risking by doing it. The thing is, he might be prepared, and even willing, to lose his life, but there is no damned reason he should." Her voice turned hard and cold. I could see barely suppressed fury rising up behind her eyes.

"Lose his life? They can't kill him." I sat up straighter, my voice becoming shrill as panic gurgled up inside me. I was angry with Jarrett. I even hated him a little for making me love him and not returning the feeling. But I didn't want him to die. I might have wished he'd let me bleed out instead of dooming me to a life of loneliness and loss, but I knew deep inside, he'd done what he'd felt was right. And in the same position, I may have done the same thing, no matter who the injured person had been. He didn't deserve to be punished for that. And most certainly not executed.

"Yes, they can," Fiona said, spearing me with an icy stare. "Look, I know you are going through something, and I promised—we all promised—Luca not to upset you, but I don't have the luxury of being soft right now. Later, you can sit in the dark and sulk or cry and rage at me all you want. But Jarrett is about to walk into that tribunal and face the death sentence. If you aren't there to testify, he won't have a chance."

"I don't..." I stopped because I had no idea what I was going to say. That I didn't want to go, that I didn't know if I could face him after yesterday, that I didn't want him to be executed? All of those things were equally true.

As if reading my mind, Fiona said, "I don't care what went down in here yesterday. I don't care what is happening between the two of you. Jarrett Campbell saved your life, and you need to get your ass up and out of that bed and do whatever you can to save his. I'll send the nurse in to help you dress. You have half an hour."

The door slammed behind her.

EIGHT
Jarrett

*A*LTHOUGH CITY HOSPITAL CATERED TO THE UPPER ranks of Nash City government employees, City Guard, and the Black Blade Guard, it wasn't the only hospital in the city, or even the largest. It hadn't even originally been built as a hospital. The building that had once held offices and stores had been chosen for its proximity to the Blade Headquarters building. Directly across the street, it had served perfectly for the initial needs of the Blades when they had set up shop in Nash City near the end of the Cataclysm.

Over the years, the building had been remodeled, changed, and added on to until it met the special needs of a hospital facility. There were still a few large rooms that had once been offices and seemed virtually untouched.

Jarrett sat in one such room now. From the rolling chalkboard at the back of the room and the stacks of wooden, folding chairs, he guessed it was used as a training room of some sort. A long, narrow table had been set up at one end. A dozen of the folding chairs had been placed in three neat rows in front of the table. Jarrett had taken up residence in the front row, his guard standing, ever vigilant, beside him.

The bright, overhead tubular crystal lamps that gave the hospital the same bright glow that fluorescent lights had once provided before the cataclysm were not activated. Instead, a few small, blue-tinged crystal lanterns hanging on portable stands had been placed around the room. At least the tribunal had given that much consideration to Anya's condition. Though he imagined it had actually been a hospital official who had ordered the lamps. Probably even Luca.

At the thought of the med-mage, Jarrett's already foul mood soured. At that moment, the door opened and Fiona, Ian, Pinky, River, and Farrah came in. River and Farrah each hugged Jarrett before settling into seats in the row behind him. Ian and Pinky shook Jarrett's hand in turn and took chairs on either side of the two young women in the second row.

"How are you doing?" Fiona asked, taking her place

in the seat next to Jarrett as one of the accused.

"I've been better, but I've been worse," Jarrett said. It was as close to the truth as he could get right now. In all honesty, he didn't really know how he was feeling. He'd been numb since walking out of Anya's room yesterday. He hadn't known if he should be hurt or angry at her rejection, so he'd opted for neither. He'd pushed out everything except the possible outcomes of today's tribunal. He didn't fear execution—not with the circumstances and witnesses. But he knew there would be consequences, and they would be as dire as the High Tribunal deemed necessary to detour any like behavior in the future, be it from him, or any other Blade. So he'd spent his every waking moment over the past twenty-four hours—which had been every moment—preparing himself.

"How are you doing?" he asked Fiona. He wasn't worried about himself, but he was concerned about Fiona. Her life wasn't in jeopardy, but her career was. And other than her family, her career was her life.

"I'm good," she said, her tone light but with an edge.

"How's Anya?" He'd had to ask. She may want nothing to do with him, but he hadn't lost his feelings for her quite so quickly.

Fiona rolled her eyes. "Annoying and whiny, but she'll live."

"Fiona," Pinky hissed over their shoulders.

Fiona turned and gave him an unapologetic grin. "Well, she is. And yeah, I get that she has reason to be. But I'm not going to coddle her. Once she snaps out of it, she'd be pissed at me if I did."

Pinky opened his mouth, then shut it and sat back in his seat.

Before Jarrett could think of anything to say, the door opened again and Luca walked in, pushing Anya in front of him in a wheelchair. Behind him, Sam and three Blade agents walked in. Jarrett recognized them as an archer and two medics who had been with them at the airship field the night Anya had been injured.

The three agents sat in the back row. Sam took the seat next to Jarrett opposite Fiona, leaving one chair empty on the front row. Luca rolled Anya, who looked tired and pale, to the front row. He moved the empty chair and pushed Anya into place next to Fiona, then pulled the displaced chair next to her wheelchair and sat next to her.

"Sir, I need you to move to the back row, please," the Blade agent who had been acting as Jarrett's guard said. He'd obviously been given precise instructions on tribunal procedure.

Luca gave the man a hard look. "I am the administrator of this facility, as well as this woman's healer. This hearing is being held against my recommendation, and I will stay by my patient's side."

Taken aback, the guard gave Sam a furtive look. The Blade Commander gave the Blade agent an almost imperceptible nod.

Wordlessly, the agent turned and walked to the door. He went out into the hall, dropped two swift knocks on the opposite door, and then stood back. A few seconds later, the other door opened. Three women and a man filed out. They walked across the hall and into the meeting room with the Blade agent following behind. The agent shut the door and took his post next to it as sentry.

The man and two of the women, each wearing long, black robes with crimson trimming and carrying a folder, sat behind the table. The third woman, the tribunal's clerk, was carrying a pad of paper and sat at a smaller table Jarrett hadn't noticed in the far corner.

The tribunal was called to order, and the clerk read a list of charges against Fiona and Jarrett. Once the charges were read, Sam stood.

"Your Honors, I would like to respectfully ask for the charges against these two agents be dropped and the full force of the law brought against me. I take full responsibility for all actions of the agents involved."

One of the judges, a woman who looked to be in her mid-thirties with short, black hair and piercing black eyes said, "Sit down, Sam. It seems that every single party involved, except for the medics and the agent who was perched on a roof nearby, claims all responsibility. Hell, despite the fact that your statement of the events exactly matches that of your agents, they both claim you were too far away to know what was happening."

Sam sat with an audible growl that promised Jarrett and Fiona a good cussing when all was said and done.

"With that in mind, we decided not to hear testimony today," another judge, a man with dark hair that was going gray at the temples, said. "Instead, the clerk has gone over all the statements of the parties involved and has put together a likely representation of events. She will read it, and you will each be given an opportunity to correct any mistakes."

The clerk came forward and began reading from her pad of paper. Jarrett listened closely as she gave a factual, if impersonal, account of the events from Anya's kidnapping to Jarrett slicing open his own wrists to save her.

Chills ran over him, hearing the details of that night read so coolly. It was as if he were listening to a tale of something that had happened to someone else. Other people that he didn't know had experienced those horrors, saw the blood, and felt their hearts being ripped out. While part of his mind heard every fact and knew it was correct, another part of him wanted to reject everything that was being said.

"Does anyone dispute the facts presented or have any other relevant facts to include?" the third judge, a curvy blond woman with bright, intelligent, blue eyes, asked.

The room was silent. Jarrett stole a glance at Anya, but her eyes were glued to her hands in her lap.

"Very well," the first judge said. "Anya Moon, are you able to stand?"

Luca made a noise, but Anya cut him off before he could get any words out.

"Yes, Your Honor," she said. It took a moment, but she pushed herself to her feet and stood straight, if a bit wobbly, in front of her wheelchair.

"Miss Moon, in your statements to Blade Agents, you have declared your wish to absolve Agent Jarrett Campbell from any wrongdoing when he knowingly and willingly infected you with the N-V virus. Is that correct?"

"Yes. Agent Campbell was only doing what he felt was right by saving my life. Neither he nor Agent Moon should be affected negatively by their actions," Anya said, her voice quiet but strong.

"I see," the judge said. "And you have signed a waiver requesting Agent Campbell be released from his one-year obligation as your guardian."

"Yes, that is correct. I don't think Agent Campbell should be pulled away from his duties to babysit me for a year. My father is willing to perform the task of guardian."

The blonde magistrate pulled a paper from her folder and slid it to the other woman. The judge looked it over, and then said, "That would be your adopted father, Eric Pinkerton?"

"Yes, Your Honor."

"I see. Miss Moon, please be seated. Eric Pinkerton, please rise."

Pinky stood from his spot directly behind Anya, reaching forward to place a hand on her shoulder as she sat. "Yes, Your Honor?"

The magistrate peered at him for a moment, and then back at the paper she held. "This says you were infected with N-V Pre-Cataclysm. And you have been legal guardian of Miss Moon since she was abandoned seventeen years ago. Is that correct?"

Pinky nodded. "Yes, your honor, though I think it has been closer to eighteen years."

"Mr. Pinkerton, have you infected any person with N-V since the enactment of the vampiric laws as set forth by the Paranorm Council of Elders? Either pre-Cataclysm or since the alliance of the Nash city-state and the Paranorm Council of Elders?"

Jarrett watched as Pinky's jaw worked, his hands clenching into fists. He expected his voice to be hard or agitated when he spoke, but it wasn't.

"Your Honors," Pinky said, smoothly addressing the entire tribunal. "I have never infected another human with the N-V virus, either legally or illegally. However, I am well versed in the laws, and I am well aware of the rules and expectations of guardianship. I freely and willingly take on the responsibility of guardianship of my daughter, Anya Moon."

Jarrett barely suppressed a grin. Pinky couldn't have answered more formally and accurately if he were a lawyer or magistrate himself.

"Thank you, Mr. Pinkerton. You can have a seat. The High Tribunal will confer for a moment. Please remain seated and silent."

With that, all three judges turned their backs to the room, the male judge, obviously a mage, said a spell, and the room fell into silence broken only by shuffling and moving in chairs.

Once again, Jarrett tried to catch a glimpse of Anya's face, but she kept her head turned towards Luca. Jarrett felt a hand on his shoulder and turned to see Pinky leaned forward, his hand on Jarrett's shoulder in a gesture of comfort and solidarity. His expression was understanding and commiserating. He may not know what happened between Jarrett and Anya, but it was clear the other vampire understood that the two of them were not on good terms any more. Jarrett thought that Pinky might be a little sad about it.

The tribunal judges turned back to the room and lifted the spell that kept their words private. Clearing his throat, the male judge said, "We are ready to give judgment."

All the shuffling stilled, and the only sound in the room was the clerk writing on her pad of paper.

The dark-haired judge said, "We accept the petition to release Agent Jarrett Campbell from his guardianship of Anya Moon."

A collective sigh of relief went up in the audience, but Jarrett wasn't sure what he felt was relief. Despite the fact that Anya wanted nothing to do with him, he still felt the need to be near her, to watch over her. He guessed it was guilt, but he couldn't seem to make it go away.

The magistrate continued to talk. "However, we reject the petition to grant full guardianship to Eric Pinkerton."

"I don't understand. Why not?" Anya's voice was shrill.

Jarrett winced. Speaking out of turn in a High Tribunal hearing could have dire consequences. Not even Fiona dared do it.

The magistrate pursed her lips. "Because we do not feel you are taking this situation seriously enough, as is evidenced by your outburst. Please refrain from speaking in this proceeding unless asked a question."

Silence.

Jarrett looked over and saw Fiona's hand tucked around Anya's, either in comfort or to try to keep her in check. An almost uncontrollable need to do the same charged through him, but Luca was on her other side, holding her other hand. Pinky and River were each leaning in from behind her, their hands on her shoulders.

A two-ton realization brick dropped on his head. Something that should have been apparent from the moment he'd laid eyes on Anya—had been apparent but he'd chose to ignore it—slammed into him like a punch to the face. There was no room for him in Anya Moon's life. There certainly hadn't been before, when she'd been a norm. And now that she was a vampire, there still wasn't. There never would be.

"Now, if we can proceed," the magistrate continued. "It is our judgment that Eric Pinkerton will have limited, joint guardianship of the yearling vampire, Anya Moon." She looked directly at Pinky. "Mr. Pinkerton, you will be responsible for making sure your daughter learns the special rule of law vampires must abide by, both civilly and personally. In other words, teach her control over body and emotions as well. You will be held accountable for your daughter's education and her actions over the next year. However, it is our feeling that as you do not directly bear the responsibility for her infection, neither should you bear the full responsibility for adherence to the vampiric laws."

"And frankly, we are not convinced that Miss Moon fully understands the seriousness of her situation or the extremely special consideration she has been given in this matter," the male judge said, his voice hard. "It is the order of this court that Anya Moon be remanded to the custody of the Nash City Black Blade Guard for the period of one year."

NINE
Jarrett

A COLLECTIVE GASP FROM EVERY PERSON IN THE audience, including Jarrett, filled the room. Sam gave a small groan that sounded suspiciously like a growl. The blonde judge shot him a quelling glare.

"She will be under the direct supervision and guardianship of Commander Sam Harrison," the dark-haired female judge continued, ignoring the mumblings. "Mr. Pinkerton, you will have full access to your daughter, but she will reside on Black Blade Guard property and be under Blade guard and surveillance at all times. Is that understood?"

"Yes, Your Honor." Pinky's answer was correct, but his voice was tense.

"I presume you are Healer Luca Jensen?" The judge gave Luca a pointed stare.

He stood. "Yes, I am."

"You will remain the head of Miss Moon's medical case. You are to appoint a psych-mage to start treatment immediately, and when Miss Moon's physically able to leave the controlled environment of this hospital, you are to remand her to the custody of the Black Blade Guard."

From the look on Luca's face he wasn't any happier about the turn of events than Jarrett, but he nodded and tersely replied, "Yes, Your Honor."

"Stop talking about me as if I'm not here." Anya's voice rang loud in the room. It was high and shrill, on the verge of panic. She pushed out of her chair, shrugging off the hands that tried to calm and restrain her.

Fiona stood, moving towards her sister to restrain her, but the blonde judge held up her hand. "Have a seat, Agent Moon. If you have something to say, now is the time to say it, Miss Moon."

Jarrett groaned inwardly, knowing the invitation to be a trap. The blonde judge was the vampire of the tribunal. And though he'd never met her, he knew she was quite old. He could see it in her eyes. She had a sweet voice and demure appearance, but her eyes were calculating. She was giving Anya enough rope to hang herself.

"I don't understand why I'm being put in jail. I did nothing wrong, and neither did anyone else." Anya's voice kept rising until she was screaming, her arms flailing like a child having a tantrum. "This is stupid and unfair."

The vampire judge nodded at Luca, who was on the edge of his seat. He shot out of his chair and pushed a needle into Anya's neck. She gasped, but then slumped against the med-mage. Fiona rose and helped him get her seated.

Once Anya was settled, the blonde judge spoke. "Miss Moon, can you hear and understand me?"

Anya's voice was groggy. "Yes."

The vampire looked to Luca.

He nodded. "The sedative calms, but she should still be able to remember and process what is happening and said to her."

"Very good," the blonde said. "Miss Moon, as you have demonstrated here, the vampiric change is nothing to take lightly. It is not just a change of body, but of mind and spirit as well. For a vampire, it takes a great deal of discipline and control to live among civilized society. It is exponentially harder for a yearling vampire. This is why the vampiric laws were put in place centuries before the Cataclysm, and why they are still so important today.

"You are being remanded to the custody of the

Black Blade Guard because both your statement to the investigating agents and your actions here today show that you have neither a proper understanding of or respect for the laws or why they are in place. Fair does not enter into the equation, Miss Moon. Although, I do believe we have been more than fair. Were it not for the special circumstances in this case, and the intervention of the High Tribunal, under Nash City law, you and all parties involved in the illegal N-V infection would have been executed.

"As you do not seem to understand the consequences of breaking laws, especially those that are so important to maintain a civilized society, your one-year confinement to Blade custody is for your own safety. Perhaps as you learn to control your body and emotions, you will also have time to ponder on the prudence of obeying all laws, not just those that are convenient and you think are fair."

A tense silence fell over the room for one long moment before the dark-haired judge spoke, "Miss Moon, you are dismissed from these proceedings. You may go back to your room and rest."

"I don't understand," Anya protested weakly, her words starting to slur. "What about Fiona and Jarrett? What will happen to them?"

"That is not your concern," the judge said. She looked at the room in general and raised her voice. "I want this room cleared of all but Black Blade Guard personnel, immediately."

Once the civilians were out of the room, it took less than ten minutes for the High Tribunal to mete out their punishment to Fiona and Jarrett. Fiona was suspended from the Blades for six months. Jarrett was sentenced to five years at a prison work camp.

He was taken directly from the hearing to the holding cells in the Blades building, not able to return to his room. He didn't have to stay in the cramped cement room for long. Within two hours, he was escorted to a visitation room to say his goodbyes to Fiona before boarding the airship that would take him to his home for the next five years.

"This is so wrong. You shouldn't be punished for saving Anya's life." Fiona paced the small holding room, her arms flailing as she raged.

Ian grabbed her by one wrist, pulling her into his arms. "Fiona, you have to calm down."

Jarrett winced, expecting Fiona to bloody Ian's nose for the remark. But to his surprise, she leaned against the necromancer and let him lead her to a chair to sit. Jarrett realized Fiona must really be in love because had any other man said those words to her, himself included, she would have knocked them unconscious.

Hoping to help bring the tension in the room down a notch, Jarrett sat at the table across from Fiona while Ian stood behind her, his hands on her shoulders.

"Fiona, I know you are upset, but try not to be. It's a damned sight better than what could have been ordered," Jarrett said.

He immediately regretted his words when Fiona looked away, but not before he saw a tear slide down her cheek. He wanted to kick himself. Reminding her that he could have been executed probably wasn't the best thing he could have said. Sometimes, he was a real idiot.

He reached across the table and took her hand. "This isn't really as bad as it seems. Five years really isn't all that long to me. You know that. Sam and I have taken precautions, so I will be okay."

She looked back at him, her eyes narrowed. "Precautions? What kind of precautions?"

"The verdict wasn't a surprise," Ian said. "They had to do something, make some sort of example of him, to deter future transgressions."

Fiona turned her gaze on Ian. "I know that. But what do you know about it? Did you have something to do with these *precautions*?"

"I did," Ian said.

Jarrett had to give it to the guy; he stood strong

in the face of his own destruction. He'd just admitted to keeping a secret from Fiona and hadn't batted an eyelash.

"And you didn't feel I needed to know?" she asked, her tone deceptively calm.

Ian shook his head. "No. You've had too much to worry about as it is. You've barely left the hospital long enough to clean up and change clothes. You've been sick with worry about your sister, and you were already worried about what might happen to Jarrett. I didn't feel like you needed anything extra on your plate. And believe it or not, we menfolk can handle things without you once in a while."

Jarrett leaned back in his seat to avoid being splashed with blood, but Fiona just stared at Ian for a long moment, her eyes narrowed, before she tilted her head and gave a little nod.

"Okay. What are these precautions you and Sam took?" she asked, turning her attention back to Jarrett.

Instead of answering, he looked at Ian. "Man, how do you get away with that?"

Ian gave a leering grin and waggled his eyebrows.

"On second thought, don't tell me. I really don't want to know," he said through laughter.

Fiona reached across the table and punched him in the shoulder. "Quit being an idiot," she said, but she was laughing as hard as Jarrett and Ian.

It felt good to laugh. Jarrett wasn't sure when he last had, or when the next time would be. After a few minutes, he sobered and answered Fiona's question. "Sam had a suspicion they would sentence me to a work camp. Five years is a relatively short period. We figured we could use the time for our own purposes. Sam is sending me to The Boro."

Fiona cut him off. "How in hell is sending you to the roughest prison compound in Appalachia *taking precautions*?"

"I can take care of myself, Tiny Fee. I am an assassin, remember?"

Her eyes went skyward. "Whatever. Go on."

"The Boro is the roughest because the worst offenders get sent there. That means there are people there with a lot of information."

"So Sam is sending you in undercover? Why? I know he has the power to send you to some cushy, minimum-security work camp where you can spend your five years doing something easy like building wagons or milking cows. And sleeping in a real bed, or at least a cot. The Boro is tents and blankets on the ground."

"And be completely useless? Fiona, rough conditions don't bother me. Neither does being around cutthroats."

Fiona looked at Ian as if trying to get him to talk some sense into Jarrett.

Ian tossed up his hands. "Don't look at me; I had the same conversation with him when he and Sam came to me for help. It's what he wants."

"Okay, so what's the plan?"

"There are several open cases, including the search for Cora, that are dead in the water without any further information. Sam briefed me on them, along with the major players. Only the warden and one staff necromancer will know I'm undercover."

"Ahh, and that's where Ian was needed," Fiona said, realization dawning.

"Yep, this is where I come in. About a third of the guards at The Boro are necromancers. What better way to keep an eye on criminals than with a network of ghosts no one can see?"

Jarrett nodded. "It is pretty brilliant. As far as the inmates, guards, the tribunal, and the world are concerned, I'm serving time like any other criminal. But Ian has a guy who has some ghosts who communicate only with him. A system has been put in place for me to pass any useful information on via the ghosts, who will get it to the necromancer, who will then report to Ian."

"And, per Sam's instructions, if things start looking too dangerous, the ghost will report in and Sam will pull Jarrett out of there," Ian added.

"Okay, then. I think it's a stupid idea, but I guess

if you can get any information on Cora, it would be worth it," Fiona said.

"Don't worry about me; I'll be fine. But I do need you to do a couple of things for me," Jarrett said.

"Name it."

"First, I need you to keep an eye on The Minnow. Take her out on the river once in a while. The wards are already tuned to your bio-energy pattern, so you can board without getting killed."

Ian laughed. "That's nice to know."

Jarrett grinned. "Well, Fiona's, not yours. Fiona, you'll have to fix that. And keep the warding crystals and the crystals in the stasis chests charged. And..."

"Hang on." She left the room and came back a moment later with a pad of paper and a pencil. "Okay, tell me everything I need to do."

For half an hour, Jarrett gave Fiona a rundown on the upkeep of his boat and how to sail her. Some of it was unnecessary, as Fiona had been on the boat before. But she wasn't a sailor, and neither was Ian. It made Jarrett feel better to give detailed instructions.

When he was sure he'd covered all the bases to make sure The Minnow was well cared for, he said, "One last thing. I need you to swear to me that no one will tell Anya about the tribunal verdict."

"What?" Fiona was incredulous.

"Don't tell her. Tell her I was sent on assignment,

whatever. Don't tell her I was sent to prison."

Fiona glared at him. "I get that she has a lot going on, and maybe you don't want her to feel guilty. Hell, you feel guilty enough for all three of us. But she should know. She has a right to know. And frankly, I think knowing she isn't the only one going through hell will help her pull her head out of her ass."

"Stop. Just don't tell her, please."

"Are you going to tell me what happened between the two of you that made her go from asking about you to not speaking to anyone in a matter of minutes?"

Jarrett shook his head, standing his ground. "No."

Fiona huffed out a breath. "Okay, I won't tell her. But I want to be on the record as saying it is a major cock-up not telling her. I won't be a part of the fallout if she finds out she was lied to. She might be pissed at you for whatever reason right now, but I know my sister. If she finds out later that you went to prison because of her and chose not to tell her, she will be livid."

If she ever got back to her 'right' frame of mind. Jarrett knew that becoming a vampire changed a person on levels deeper than the physical. Anya may never be the fun-loving, ready-to-smile girl she'd been just a couple of weeks ago. And that was his fault. But it wasn't something he needed to say to Fiona. She held out hope her sister would get through this somewhat unscathed, and he wasn't about to take that away from her.

"Fine, if she finds out, I'll take full responsibility," he said. It wouldn't matter. He couldn't make Anya hate him any more than she already did.

A knock sounded, and a Blade agent opened the door. "It's time to go."

The three of them stood. Suddenly, Jarrett was knocked back a step as Fiona hurled herself at him. He wrapped his arms around her as she hugged him.

"Thank you for saving my sister. You be safe."

He dropped a kiss on the top of her head. "You are so welcome. And don't worry, Tiny Fee. I'll be just fine."

She pulled away from him, swiping a hand across her face in a futile attempt to hide the dampness. "You better. Or I'll kick your ass."

TEN
Anya
Three Months Later

I WAS SEATED AT THE LARGE, TREADLE SEWING MACHINE in my sitting room when a loud knock sounded. "Who is it?" I pointlessly called. I only ever saw three people, and only two of those came to my room. My weekly medical checkup with Luca had been just two days ago and he always called before stopping by, so it had to be Pinky for his daily visit.

"Your father."

Great. He sounded annoyed. As if that were something different these days. I knew he didn't mind the daily visits or the mandatory 'training' he had to do with me, teaching me to control my heightened emotions and impulses so that I wouldn't be a danger to society. But I wasn't as eager a pupil as he wished, and it had him in a state of constant frustration.

"Come in," I called back. I didn't bother to get up. Instead, I continued to concentrate on the rocking motion of my feet on the treadle and feeding the material under the needle.

"Your attitude needs work, young lady," Pinky said,

"Tell me something I don't know," I said, my tone bored as I continued to sew the skirt. Not that I needed a new one. I had sewn dozens in the past three months, along with shirts, dresses, and corsets.

Sewing was the only thing that kept my mind off the constant buzz of energy that flowed through my body. The rhythmic rocking motion of my feet on the treadle, the hum of the rotating wheel, and the steady click of the needle as it plunged in and out of the fabric calmed me. I concentrated on it instead of the disappointed tones in Pinky's voice, until the machine clattered to an abrupt stop. I looked over to see Pinky's hand on the wheel that moved the needle.

"Hey..."

"Don't 'hey' me," he said, his voice stern. "We need to talk, and that means you need to pay attention to me."

I pushed back from the machine and went to settle on the settee that dominated the sitting room, preparing myself for whatever lecture he was giving today.

Pinky didn't sit. Instead, he paced the length of the room. "I had a meeting with Psych-Mage Misra today."

I groaned, knowing immediately what his disappointment was about today. "Look," I said, cutting him off at the pass. "I know what you are going to say, but I'll tell you like I told her, I don't want to do the memory regression. It's pointless."

"Misra believes it will help you cope better with your situation. And so do I."

"I'm fine," I said.

"No, Anya, you're not," he said, his voice carefully measured as if he were struggling not to raise his voice. "You mope around here like a pouting three-year-old. You do nothing but sew all day. You refuse to see your sisters. You won't talk about your feelings in your therapy sessions, and you won't talk about them with me. You are barely cooperative in our emotional training sessions. You've closed yourself off from everyone and everything. It's not healthy."

I let out a derisive snort. "I don't need to talk about what happened, or about my feelings. Considering the fact that I was kidnapped, nearly murdered, changed into a vampire without my permission, and then arrested, I think I'm doing a bang-up job at dealing with my *situation*."

Pinky let out an exasperated sigh, so heavy I could almost see the moment his control snapped. He turned on me, his face tight with anger.

"I get it. I really do. Having your entire life turned inside out sucks, hardcore. I've been there, done that, and threw away the bloody T-shirt. You are entitled to be sad, angry, and confused. For a little while. But it's been three months and your pissy attitude is getting a tad bit old. It's time to suck it up, buttercup, and get on with your life." Pinky punctuated his rant by crossing his arms over his chest and giving me a stare that dared me to yell back at him. I took him up on it.

"I'm in fucking jail, in case you didn't notice. I didn't do a fucking thing wrong, and I've been locked up like a criminal," I screamed.

"Don't be such a whiner, Anya. Boo-fucking-hoo. You're not in jail, and you very well could be."

I took a step back, shocked by Pinky's words. They sounded more like something Fiona would say. Pinky, even when disciplining us, had always been kind. This Pinky wasn't kind, sympathetic, or anything I'd come to expect from him. It made it easier to scream back at him, my hurt and anger making my voice shrill.

"Not in jail? Look around. I'm confined to these rooms. There's a guard in the next room, for fuck's sake."

The two rooms I occupied were actually part of a three-room suite, three rooms in a line, but the front room, the one that opened onto the hall, was the dominion of the guard on duty who was tasked with keeping an eye on me. There was a rotation of five or six of them, but I didn't bother learning their names. I had no interest in chatting it up with my jailers.

Pinky closed his eyes for a moment, shaking his head gently as if trying to muster strength. When he opened his eyes and spoke, his tone was one of tired exasperation. "Yes, Anya, there's a guard outside of this spacious two-room suite with attached restroom. Do you know why?"

Of course I knew why. What was I—an idiot child? "Because the Tribunal ordered my incarceration for my first year as a vampire," I spat out, the "duh" at the end silent.

"Yes, the tribunal ordered you to be taken into custody and held for one year. I may not work in law enforcement like your sister does, but I do know what that usually means. Any other person would have been thrown into one of the concrete holding cells below ground, let out only for mandatory therapy. Human contact would have been limited to a therapist, vampire mentor, and if needed, a med-mage. None of which would be your friends or family."

He paused, waiting for a reaction, but I just glared at him.

His eyes narrowed, and he went on. "You really don't understand what has been done for you, do you? Instead of throwing you in lockup for a year, Sam has gone out of his way to make you comfortable. You are in a cozy suite of rooms usually reserved for Blade agents and visiting government officials.

"You can have any visitors you like; any time you like. You have a sewing machine, books, a scry crystal—everything you need to make this place your home for a year."

"A gilded cage is still a cage."

Drawing in deep breath, he let it out in an exasperated groan. "Anya, there isn't a lock on your door keeping you confined in here. Instead, Sam is spending Blade resources to give you a guard twenty-four hours a day. You can leave the room, even the building, and go anywhere you want. You just have to take a guard with you. He has bent, twisted, and mutilated the law in every way possible to make this year as easy on you as possible, and you stand there, whining like a spoiled brat. I didn't raise you to be like this."

"Don't you get it? I can't be who you raised me to be. I'm not that person anymore. I don't know who I am." Anger and frustration burst out of me in the form of flooding tears and body-wracking sobs.

In an instant, Pinky was next to me, grabbing me and pulling me into his arms. I sank into him just as I had when I was a child. He gently guided me over to the sofa and we sat, my head buried in his chest, as he stroked my hair.

"Something has to change," he said when I'd finally stopped crying and sat up, grabbing a nearby scrap of cloth to wipe my face. "You can't go on like this. Sewing was a great start. It gave you something to pass the time, but it doesn't seem to be enough. You have stacks and stacks of clothes you'll never wear. I doubt your savings will be intact much longer if you keep sending orders to River for more fabric. You need to get out of these rooms. You need to find something to focus on that gives you purpose."

"What do you suggest I do? I'm a bartender. Was a bartender. But I can't work in the pub because I might get mad and throw a glass at someone's head," I said, frustration rising again.

"Much the same reason we don't let Fiona tend bar. But unlike her, you will learn to control your emotions eventually," he teased.

I laughed. A vampire Fiona was too scary to contemplate. "I hope so. But what then? Do you and I run the pub together for the rest of eternity?"

He shrugged. "I don't know Anya. I know the pub is where I belong; it is my happy place. You always have a place there. It is and will always be your home. But I don't know that it is your happy place. You'll have to find that on your own."

"And what if I never do? I feel like everything has

been ripped apart, and I don't know how to go about gluing it back together."

"You can start by visiting with your sisters. They miss you."

I stiffened and pulled away from him, pacing to the other side of the room, my back to him. "I can't. I don't want to. I just can't handle it."

"I get it," Pinky said, his tone relaxed and full of understanding. "I understand what it's like to watch the people you love age every single day, knowing that someday, way too soon, they are going to die. I've buried more loved ones than I care to count. I go through my life every day knowing I'll have to add my daughters to that list someday. The pain could be crippling, if I let it. But trust me when I tell you, letting the fear of that inevitable loss keep you from the people you love and who love you isn't just unfair to them. It's unfair to yourself. By shutting them out of your life, you miss out on the joyous moments. And I promise, those moments are the ones that stay with you forever, long after the pain of loss has faded."

His words hit me square in the heart. I took a deep breath, determined not to let tears take hold again. I would not let my emotions debilitate me.

"I feel like they are already lost to me, and seeing them just twists the knife. I don't know how to make that feeling go away," I said, staring at the wall.

I heard Pinky stand. "The first step is therapy. But the therapy only works if you cooperate with your psych-mage. You need to take her advice."

"You mean memory regression." I made a derisive noise. The conversation had come full circle.

"Yes, memory regression. You can scoff at it all you want, but you can't move forward until you face what happened to you."

I clenched my fists at my side. "I have nothing to face. I know everything I need to know. A psycho bitch kidnapped me, she cut my throat, and I was infected with the N-V virus to save me. Case closed." I didn't need to remember every gory detail.

"Anya, it's not..."

"I said no," I snapped, my voice cold.

Letting out an exasperated sigh, Pinky said, "I can see we aren't going to get past this today. I'm going to go, but I want you to think seriously about what I said. Your sisters want to see you; they need to see you. And so does Farrah. I think it would do her a world of good."

I dropped my head, shame washing over me at Farrah's name. Since my abduction, she had not been doing well. Pinky had told me that she was suffering from post-traumatic stress disorder. Though she was helping out around the pub more, and had pretty much taken over my spot as bartender, she was much more quiet and reserved than she had been before and hadn't left the pub in the three months since she'd been released from the hospital. While my incarceration was tribunal-imposed, hers was more out of her control. Pinky had told me that every time she tried to walk out the door, or anyone talked about her going out, she had a panic attack. She was seeing a psych-mage, just as I was, but no progress had been made.

"I'll think about it," I lied.

I felt awful about Farrah's situation. It was all my fault. I knew I should talk to her, apologize or something, but I couldn't. Although I wasn't as close to her as I was to my sisters, I did care about her. That made her one more person I'd lose. When I thought about it, a tight ball formed in my chest, making it hard to breathe. I wondered if that was how Farrah felt when she thought about going outside.

"I'll see you tomorrow." Pinky's tone told me he knew I was lying, but that he wouldn't press the issue anymore today. Walking over, he dropped a kiss on my cheek and left.

ELEVEN
Anya

AFTER PINKY LEFT, I TRIED TO GET BACK TO SEWING, but I was too agitated. It was my normal state these days. I wanted to punch something or someone. But I couldn't get my frustrations out by fighting anymore. I wouldn't be allowed to fight at Pete's or any of the other fight houses I frequented since I wasn't a norm anymore. There were vampire fight houses, sure, but the rules, and Nash City law, didn't allow yearling vamps to participate. Even if I weren't under twenty-four hour guard, there would be nowhere I could go.

Instead, I resorted to what little exercise I could get in my little room. I did pushups, sit-ups, and jumping jacks in an effort to release excess energy. I was running in place when a knock sounded on my door. When I flung it open, I found Luca standing on the other side, smiling.

"Did Pinky send you here to check up on me? If so, you can just hit the road because I don't need a healer or another shrink," I snapped.

Luca's smile didn't falter. Unaffected by my rudeness, he said, "I haven't seen Pinky in a few days. I came because I missed your smiling face, but since you don't seem to have one anymore, I'd say I'm here in concerned friend capacity."

Shame flooded my being. I sighed and stepped back, giving him access to my room. "I'm sorry; I'm just a little cranky. Please come in."

He strode in as if he owned the place. Pulling the chair away from the sewing machine, he sat down, straddling it so that his arms rested on the back. "Tell me what has you all fired up, cranky-pants."

I sighed. Going over to the stasis cabinet in the corner, I pulled out a bottle of blood. "Want?"

He shook his head. "Nah, not hungry."

I drank half the bottle down, then put it back in the cabinet. The crystals attached to the inside walls of the cabinet were charged with a spell that literally stopped time inside the cabinet. It was excellent for keeping food, including blood, fresh.

"Pinky and I got into it," I said, flopping back down

on the sofa. "He started in on me, again, about needing to find focus. He says the sewing isn't enough."

Luca's eyes scanned the room, taking in the piles of clothes, fabric, and baskets of thread and sewing supplies. "I can't say I disagree with him on the sewing part. It's starting to get out of control in here."

"Not a lot else I can do since I can't join the City Guard or the Blades."

"Did you tell Pinky? About asking Sam about joining the Blades, I mean," Luca asked.

I shook my head. "Why bother? The rule is that a vampire has to be changed at least a decade before they will be considered for entry into the academy for either City Guard or Blade training. There's nothing to be done, so why even tell Pinky?"

"And you are sure there's no way to bypass that since you already have all the pre-requisite law courses from when you attended the academy before?" he asked.

"No. Sam scryed me yesterday to let me know. Exceptions can be made if the commanders of the City Guard, the Blades, and the Academy's chancellor all agree. And they do. However, because I'm still a yearling, the Paranorm Council, or rather their liaisons, have to sign off on it."

Realization dawned on Luca's face. "And in this case, those liaisons are the judges of the High Tribunal."

I huffed out a sigh. "And so you see the problem.

Sam went to them, but they said I didn't have enough self-control to be allowed to even sit in a classroom with other students, much less combat train with them. Not that they are wrong. I never know from one minute to the next if I'll be sobbing like a baby or rampaging. Or what will trigger a mood swing."

"Anya, it takes time. You've only been a vampire a few months. It can take a while to get used to the hormonal changes. The one-year guardianship law was put into place for a reason. Even then, it can take years, even decades, to learn the control you had as a norm."

Despite his soothing tone, a red-hot ball of rage formed in my stomach. "I will not spend decades twiddling my thumbs and cooling my heels tending bar."

"I thought you enjoyed working at Pinky's," he said smoothly.

A little bit of the wind went out of my sails. "I did. I enjoy the customers and I love Pinky. But it was always my fallback job. It was what I did because I couldn't be a City Guard, much less my ultimate goal, a Blade. But I know that it won't be enough now. Pinky understands that. He said as much today."

"Actually, I understand it, too," he said. "But, Anya, not getting into Guard training right away doesn't mean you'll be stuck working at the pub for long. You work on your control this year, and when you are free to go back to work, train part time until you can get into the academy training course."

"Not good enough," I snapped. I would not wait that long to go after Cora. I just couldn't. I would go mad. But I couldn't say that. Although I'd confided in Luca how much I wanted to join the City Guard and eventually become a Black Blade Guard agent, I hadn't told him exactly why. He'd assumed it was because that had always been my dream, but it had been denied me before because of my status as a norm. I'd let him go on assuming, knowing he wouldn't approve of my desire to hunt down Cora and kill her.

"Luca, I don't expect you to understand, but training to become a Guard isn't my ultimate goal. I don't even really want to be a City Guard. It's actually a means to an end. I want to join the Black Blade Guard, but I have a goal that goes beyond even that. Once I enter the training course, it will still take several years to become a Blade. I can't sit around for five or ten years before even starting the process. I just can't."

The last part came out in a frustrated sob and I sank down, further into the sofa, tears streaming down my cheeks. In the past few months, I'd gotten over the embarrassment I would have once felt if anyone, even family, had seen me cry. Dealing with extreme mood swings and intense emotions that came with vampirism had taught me that crying wasn't a sign of weakness, but a release of energy. I still had very little control of my outbursts, but tears were better than breaking someone's arm. That was progress.

Luca rose from his chair and came to sit down next to me, taking my hand in his. "Anya, my changing wasn't like yours. I chose to be infected with the N-V virus knowing the full consequences and with plenty of time to prepare. But even so, I do understand what you are going through, at least in part."

I turned my head so I could look at him through watery eyes. I could see the compassion and empathy in his face, but I couldn't imagine how he could possibly understand how I felt right now. The elation at finally having the opportunity to have the career I always wanted dampened by the inability to actually have that career for many more years. The sorrow of knowing one day my sisters would be gone, the hole blasted in my heart by Jarrett, and this consuming, driving need to make Cora pay for bringing so much pain and upheaval to my life and those I love were so meshed together into a tight ball of fury and anguish. How could Luca, or anyone, understand it when I couldn't?

"Will you tell me about your life before you were changed?" I asked, my voice tremulous.

He scooted back on the sofa so that he was leaning against the arm, a pillow behind him, and patted his chest. "Come snuggle with me, baby girl."

I did as he said, crawling up next to him and settling in the small space between him and the back of the sofa. He put his arm around me and I laid back, my head nestled on his shoulder. Almost immediately, a pulse of warm calmness washed over me. I felt more comfortable and relaxed than I had since before my encounter with Cora. It was wonderful. I wanted to sink down against Luca and enjoy the feeling, yet I knew it was odd to feel this way.

"What are you doing?" I asked hesitantly.

"It's one of my gifts."

"One of your powers? Did you get it when you were changed?"

"No, but it was definitely enhanced. If you'll lay back and let me help you relax, I'll tell you the whole, long story."

I sank into him, letting whatever soothing power he had wash over me. "Okay, tell the story."

"You know I was born only a few years before the start of the Cataclysm, right?"

"Yeah, you are about fifty or sixty years younger than Pinky, I think."

He laughed. "Yeah, but I think Pinky was about a decade and a half younger than me when he was changed. I was just three months shy of my thirty-fifth birthday when I was infected."

"Still look young and sexy to me." I grinned.

"You're not wrong, baby girl." He winked.

I laughed, genuinely amused. It was the first time in a while, and it felt good. "Have you always been this smooth, or did it come with old age?"

"Baby, I was born with game. Though in truth, I didn't get a lot of chances to practice it in my early years. I was too busy with medical school."

"Medical school? Is that like the academy?"

He shook his head, one side of his mouth quirking up. "Not even close. Becoming a doctor, a norm version of a med-mage, was a long, difficult process. Anyway, the Cataclysm, though it wasn't called that at the time, really started to show by the time I was in college. Though the weather changes and natural disasters had been increasingly more erratic, most people, especially world leaders, denied it was happening. The scientists called it climate change."

"What was it like?"

"Beyond anything you can imagine. Though not at first. It was a gradual thing. But by my second year in college, there was no more denying something was happening. Though the scientists had theories about the magnetic polar shift, there was nothing that could be done. Not even by mages. It got worse and worse. You know how you feel like you never know from one moment to the next what you'll be feeling, but you know whatever it is, it will be intense?"

"Yeah. It sucks."

"That's what the weather was like. Blizzards in the middle of summer, hurricanes that were stronger than any storm ever measured. And they just kept getting stronger. There were earthquakes, volcanoes erupting, and every other type of natural disaster you could imagine. People were dying and going hungry due to crops being wiped out. But still, life was somewhat normal for most of the world. Then the wars started. Everyone blamed everyone else for the suffering."

His voice had become distant. I sat up. He was staring off into space, a haunted look on his face.

"Luca, we don't have to talk about this. You don't have to tell me."

He blinked, and then looked at me. "No, it's okay. Come here."

He motioned for me to lie back down, so I did.

"Okay, where was I? I won't go into all the details. I was in my first year of my residency—like an apprenticeship—at a hospital in New York City when the bombs started. The country was in chaos. Everyone had started evacuating big cities that might be targets, fleeing to the country and smaller towns. But my wife and I were doctors and we were needed, so we stayed in the city to keep working at the hospital."

"You were married?" I asked, not sure why that surprised me. I'd always pegged Luca as a 'settle down' type of guy.

"Lauren and I met the first day of medical school. Somehow, between all-night study sessions and tests, we fell in love. We married in the middle of all that chaos. She was a beautiful, brilliant doctor. And she wasn't half bad as a wife."

He smiled, and I was glad that talking about her didn't seem to make him sad.

As if reading my mind, he said, "I miss her, and I'd go out of my mind if I let myself think about her all the time. So I built a little box in my heart where she will forever live. And when I take her out for a little while, I can see her bright smile, her wild, curly hair that never behaved, hear her wildly inappropriate jokes, and smell her stinky farts."

I laughed so hard I snorted. "She sounds like quite a woman," I said when I could speak again.

"She was," he said, smiling. "She was a wonderful doctor. We were both at the hospital when word came in that an earthquake had hit off the coast and a devastating tsunami was headed our way. What was left of the military forces in the city came through to help evacuate patients to a field hospital inland. I rode in one truck with several critical patients. Lauren rode in the one behind us. The weather was bad; their truck got stuck in a muddy road. A tree fell on it before they could get it pulled free. Lauren was seriously injured. By the time we got everyone to the field hospital, there was nothing that could be done. She was bleeding internally. We didn't have the equipment to operate, and I wasn't a surgeon."

"But you were a med-mage."

He nodded. "Yes, I was. But my healing powers were not strong enough. Her injuries were too severe. All I could do was sit with her and use the one power I had that could help."

"Your calming ability?"

"Yes. Norms, who had no idea what magic was, always said I had an amazing bedside manner because I could settle even the most panicky patients."

I realized he must have used the power on me before; there was no telling how many times. "You used it on me that first day in the hospital, when I had the panic attack."

"Yes, I did."

"So, what happened to you next?" I asked.

"I sat holding Lauren's hand for I don't know how many hours. However long it took. In the end, we were able to control her pain, I was able to keep her calm, and she died with a smile on her face. After, I got up and walked out of the camp."

Twelve
Anya

SHOCKED, I SAT UP SO I COULD LOOK AT HIM. I STUDIED his face, but his dark eyes were unreadable.

"You just left? But you were a doctor, a magical doctor. I'm betting that even if they had other doctors there, none of them had the same abilities as you. They needed you." I winced at how accusing I sounded, but I couldn't pull the words back once they were out.

Luca didn't seem offended. He just nodded, no emotion showing. "You are right. And later, once I was able to feel again, I carried guilt over that for a very long time. But at the time, I couldn't feel anything but pain and grief.

"I was born with the powers to comfort and heal.

Mine was a mage family with roots going back to before time was recorded in writing. We were registered with the Paranorm Council, something you had to do back then. I was taught from an early age to love and respect my powers and to use them to help others, norms and paranorms alike. That is why I became a doctor.

"I could have worked as a homeopathic healer, but my reach would have been limited. I learned norm medical science so I could help more people. I could hide my healing behind medicines and still help those with illnesses and injuries I could not heal. My abilities were the one thing I'd always had faith in. But they failed me when I could not save the most important person in my life. In that moment, I had nothing. My home was underwater, I'd lost touch with my family months before when they fled the city, and then Lauren was gone because my magic hadn't been strong enough to save her. Something broke inside me."

His voice was soft and distant, cracking on the last sentence. I took his hand in mine, offering comfort, though I didn't know if it was for him or for me.

"I'm so sorry you had to go through that, Luca. But I don't understand. You were just a mage then. If you weren't infected by N-V, why would you choose that after the losses you suffered?" I couldn't even bear the thought of losing my sisters and then living for an eternity with the memories. Yet, he had lost everything and still chose to become a vampire.

He smiled at me. "It wasn't a choice I made lightly. When Lauren died, all I wanted to do was join her. I wandered, taking shelter in bombed out or abandoned buildings, scavenging supplies from homes and businesses that had been left by owners who had died or fled. I avoided other people like the plague, though occasionally, I did happen upon other travelers. When that happened, I might share a meal or information about what was going on in parts of the world they were from, but that was it."

"That sounds like a lonely existence," I said, sorrow for him hot and stinging behind my eyes.

"It was," he said. "But it was how I wanted it at the time. Somehow, I found the strength to fight to survive, but I think it was more out of punishing myself, making myself suffer because I hadn't saved Lauren."

"That's not why you chose to become a vampire, is it?" I asked, my voice quiet as I contemplated choosing to punish yourself with pain, forever.

Flashing a sweet smile, he squeezed my hand. "No, baby girl, though if the thought had occurred to me at the time, I might have. I was in a dark place, and I was not a good person for a long time. I didn't hurt anyone, but neither did I help. I came across so many people who were sick or injured, yet I never told anyone I was a doctor. I never offered my skills, never used my magic."

I tried to reconcile what he was telling me with the man I knew him to be, but I just couldn't. "Something must have changed. Because I can't imagine you not helping anyone who needed you."

"I spent two years alone. I made it to the Appalachian Mountains and just wandered, living in caves, foraging and hunting for food to survive.

"Then one night, while looking for a cave to take shelter in, I stumbled on a group of people much larger than I'd ever encountered who weren't stationary in a town. The earthquake and tsunami that sent us running from New York had been the first in what seemed to be a never-ending series of them. By that time, two years later, the entire Eastern seaboard was underwater, and it was spreading inland quickly. Whole towns were evacuating, running from the water and weather."

"So it was a group of refugees?"

"Yes. Mostly norms, except the four leaders. There were two shifters, a mage, and a vampire. And it was the first time in my life that I'd ever known paranorms to be open about who they were. They were using their abilities to help the refugees get to safety."

"All the history books and all the stories I've heard from Pinky and other vampires around the pub say the Cataclysm was why paranorms were finally able to come out of hiding without fearing persecution. Because so many stepped up to use their abilities to help others," I said.

I'd heard stories before; I'd spent most of my life in a vampire bar. But few ever actually gave details about the Cataclysm. Vampires who lived through it usually preferred not to talk about it at all. And if they had stories similar to Luca's, I could see why.

He nodded. "Yes. Apparently, it had started happening all over, but I was very out of touch. This group, the four paranorms, were going back and forth between the places that were being destroyed, flooded, and by that point, frozen in some places, and helping survivors get to safe places."

"Like Nash?" I asked, remembering how it was one of the earliest sanctuaries for Cataclysm refugees.

"Not yet, no. There weren't any sanctuary cities set up yet. The group was mainly getting people to higher ground and into the mountains where they had a chance of finding caves for shelter and hunting for food. But what they were doing was great, and the fact that they were putting themselves out there just hit something inside me."

I grinned at him. "The good part you were trying to bury."

"Maybe so. All I know is I looked at that group of refugees and the paranorms helping them, and I could hear Lauren's voice in my head. And it wasn't pretty either. She basically cussed me out; said I needed to stop feeling sorry for myself and get off my ass to help those people."

I snorted. "I think I would have liked your wife."

"Yeah, you would have. She was a lot like you, baby girl. Always quick with a smile and a joke, but never took shit from anyone."

I cast my eyes down. I didn't think I was that person anymore. But I didn't want to think or talk about me. "So you joined them?"

"I told them I was a med-mage and a doctor. I asked if I could travel with them for a while. We got the refugees to a settlement in the mountains. Refugee groups from all over came together and had taken over a network of caves, turning them into homes and safe areas. It was amazing. I knew then that I wanted to help, but I still felt a little useless. My powers just weren't strong enough to heal serious injuries or illnesses that had gone on too long."

"And that is when you decided to be changed?"

"Yes. I saw these people working together, fighting to survive, turning cold, damp caves into homes and places of sanctuary, and I knew I had to help people again. But I couldn't go through losing someone the way I lost Lauren again, just because my powers were too weak. So I asked Philip, the vampire in the group, to change me."

"Wow. Did you keep traveling with them?"

"Yes, for nearly a decade. And yes, I lost patients. But while it never got easy, and it never will, at least now I know that if a patient dies, I have done everything humanly, medically, and magically possible to save them."

"You did with Lauren, as well," I said, stroking his cheek with my fingers.

"I know that now. And I probably even knew it deep inside then, but it wasn't something I could accept." He turned his face into my hand and his lips pressed against my palm, velvet smooth, warm, and damp.

The warmth traveled up my arm and started a strange yearning that quickly spread throughout me. I dropped my hand and sat back a little.

"How do you talk about Lauren and everything that happened so matter-of-factly? I mean, you lost so much, and I can tell how much you loved her, yet there's no sadness."

He smiled at me and pulled himself up straight on the sofa. "I was sad for a very long time. I've seen more death than I care to think about, and Lauren's wasn't the first. But eventually, I realized that dwelling on the loss of her was actually a disservice to her memory and the person she was. So, like I said, I built a little box in my heart and put her in there. She will live there, bright and beautiful forever. And when I'm alone and

I want to smile, I take her out and think about all the beautiful memories we made. But before I let them get sad, I put her back in her box and I go on with my life. There are other boxes in there too. The ones filled with dark memories that never get opened again."

"Except for tonight. Thank you for that—for telling me your story."

He shot me a grin. "I told you for a reason, you know? My changing story is nothing like yours, so there's not much I can offer by way of advice on how to cope with those circumstances. But I know you lock yourself up in here to avoid the pain you get when you see your sisters. But sweetness, you can't go around avoiding pain. It will find you. You are much better off making beautiful memories to keep close to your heart. They will soothe the pain."

Hot tears pricked behind my eyes before falling, scalding, down my cheeks. "I don't know if I can."

He brushed one thumb across my cheek, wiping away the wetness. "Anya Moon, you are a lot of things, but you are not a quitter. Did you know I used to bet on your fights at Pete's?"

Startled, I shook my head. "No. I don't remember ever seeing you, but it's not exactly a vampire hangout and I'm usually busy dodging punches."

"I was in full daytime gear, so you probably wouldn't have known it was me even if you had seen me. I had been to the market, and there was an accident on the docks. After I went down to help and on my way home, I saw you go into Pete's, intending to say hi, but then you got into the ring. I watched you fight, and though I'm not much on violence—being a healer and all—I was mesmerized. It was one of the most graceful and powerful things I'd ever seen. I immediately went to Pete and put a running bet on all of "Spitfire's" fights. You've made me a ton."

I laughed, something lightening inside me. "You're welcome."

"They don't call you Spitfire just because of the color of your hair. It's your spirit, your fire. Your determination. I'm sure there were people, maybe even Pete, who said 'no, you can't fight here' when you first started, wasn't there?"

"Yes. I had to kick a lot of ass to get taken seriously and to be respected."

"Exactly. Every time you climbed into that ring with some big, ugly thug, you were refusing to take no for an answer. You were refusing to let them judge you by your gender or size. So tell me, baby girl, why are you taking no for an answer now?"

I stared at him, stunned. I couldn't have been more shocked if he'd slammed a right hook into my jaw. "I don't... I don't know what you mean."

"When I first got here tonight, you told me all about

how everyone is telling you 'No, you can't train to be a guard'. I'm just wondering—why are you taking it so meekly?"

"But the High Tribunal..."

He shook his head, cutting me off. "They said you couldn't join the City Guard cadets at the academy. But they can't prevent you from training."

"I lack control," I said, my voice sounding whiny even to my ears.

Luca's brows furrowed in confusion. "I'm not an expert in fighting, but isn't that what training is for? It seems to me that if you were focused on physical training, it would help you get control of your emotions."

I just stared at him for an eternity, thoughts racing through my brain. Maybe I couldn't start the academy yet, but could I train and get enough control to let them allow me to enroll soon? And if not, were there other options? My brain was in overdrive, and for the first time in ages, I felt like there might be possibilities for me.

I grinned at Luca. "I can't promise any overnight changes, but I promise I'll try to stop taking no for an answer. Even from myself."

His smile was sweet, bright, and gave me a strange feeling of hope. "That's my girl."

"Thank you, Luca. For calming me down, sharing your story, and being straight with me. You are an amazing friend," I said, leaning in to give him a kiss of thanks and friendship.

That was my only intention but the moment my lips touched his, flames burst inside me.

Thirteen
Anya

*H*is mouth was warm and firm against mine. I reached out my tongue, flicking it across his bottom lip. He tasted like sweet and spice, like honey laced with chili. It was intoxicating. My tongue repeated its path. This time, he opened his mouth with a groan. As the kiss deepened, I pushed up to my knees, my hands bracing on his shoulders.

One of his arms went around my waist as the other hand plunged into my hair. I moved forward until my knees were straddling his hips, and then I gave a slight push. He pulled me close and took me with him as he fell back onto the sofa until he was lying almost flat and I was on top of him. I pressed my hips down, and I could feel him hot and hard under me, separated only by the heavy denim of our pants. I twisted my hips, rubbing against him until we were both moaning and gasping into each other's mouths.

We spent an eternity like that, kissing, touching, with our hands roaming. His hand slid over my rear, pressing me harder against him, and then back up to my waist, pushing up the material of my shirt. The feel of his hand on my bare skin sent flames erupting through me.

"Anya, I want you," Luca said against my mouth, his voice deep and velvety.

"Mmmm." I wanted, too. So much. My body ached to be touched, ached for release. I wanted so much. But something wasn't right. I tried to push it out of my head, focusing instead on the feel of Luca's hand as it made its way around my stomach and up to my breast, bare under my shirt. His palm grazed my nipple, and it felt so good.

"Yes." I moaned again, arching against him. I was on fire. Yet, still, something just didn't feel right. Something was wrong.

There was a strange disconnect between my body and my brain that I'd never realized before. It was true that I'd never felt the rush of emotions I'd felt when making love with Jarrett with anyone else, yet it wasn't until this very moment that I realized how different it felt.

My body felt all the right things. My skin was flushed, adrenaline raced through my veins, and a heat pulsed between my legs. Need raced through me, hot and strong.

But there was something missing. There was no fluttering in the pit of my stomach, no quickening of my pulse at his nearness. I knew, instinctively, that it wasn't because of the vampiric changes. It was something more complicated.

Suddenly, I realized what was missing. My body had a need; it ached to have that need met. But the thing that was missing was the soul-deep craving that meant only Luca could be the one to quench the burning thirst. At this moment, almost any man could do the job, or I could even do it myself. Aside from the extreme intensity vampirism had brought to every emotion and feeling, this was exactly how sex had always felt to me. Like a hot, exciting itch that needed to be scratched. Yet never before had it felt lacking.

I gasped and pulled away from Luca, jumping off the sofa and putting as much distance between us as I could in the small room. "Luca, I can't."

"I don't understand," he said, confusion knitting his brow. "You seem pretty aroused."

Oh, I was. My body was revved up and ready to go, no doubt about it. "It's not that..."

"It's Jarrett," he said, cutting me off. "You're still in love with him."

"I... No. Yes. No. It's not that simple," I said, wringing my hands, flustered.

Luca closed the distance between us and took my hands in his, stilling them. "I know it's not, and that's okay. Whatever happened between the two of you, it will take a long time to get over. I'm not trying to step into his place. I don't want anything you can't give."

The warmth of his hands on mine were stoking the fires inside me, making me itch to throw myself back into his arms. "Are you saying you don't want to have sex with me?"

"That's so far off from what I'm saying it's not even in the same galaxy."

His laugh was rich, throaty, and sent tingles down my spine. Then those tingles spread out. The scent of him, clean and male, filled my senses, clouding my brain. I pulled my hands out of his, taking a step back. Then another. And another.

"I need to be over here so I can think. So what are you saying?"

"You are my friend, and I care deeply about you. You are stunningly sexy, and I want you like there's no tomorrow."

"Oh."

"And I'm not asking you for anything you aren't willing to give. Meaning love, or even a relationship that goes beyond friendship."

"But you want sex. So sex and friendship?" I asked.

"Yes. And I'll own up to it being one-hundred-percent selfish. I'll refer back to the wanting you like there's no tomorrow thing I said a minute ago."

I laughed, but he continued.

"But there are medical benefits as well. I'm sure Pinky discussed the specific challenges vampiric women face, and you've likely been experiencing them as well."

My eyes widened in horror. "Yes, he did, and I am not having that conversation with you."

"Anya, I'm a med-mage. That sort of thing goes with the territory."

"I don't care. No way after what just happened on that sofa am I discussing that with you. It was bad enough having to talk about it with Pinky. Worse than when I was a teenager and getting my first period." I shuddered.

I had known, intellectually, that the N-V virus caused an increase in hormones and a decrease in inhibitions, causing the vampiric sexual drive to be much stronger than that of a non-vamp. But knowing it and feeling it were two different things. It knocked me for a loop; just being in the same room with male guards had made me want to jump their bones. But it had been surprisingly easy to control. And then it wasn't easy. It was excruciating. I was in a constant state of need, and I was more irritable than I'd ever been in my life. Then Pinky explained that just because female vampires couldn't get pregnant (the virus killed viable eggs), the hormonal portion of the reproductive system still worked. It worked in super-vampiric style. Which meant that though I didn't get periods every month, I still got hypersensitive, cranky, and balls-to-the-wall horny. Every. Single. Month.

"Okay, we don't have to discuss it in detail," Luca said, still laughing. "I'll just say this, as a medical professional, not a guy who wants to get into your pants. If you want to learn to control your emotions and your body's reactions to stressors, you need to learn to work with them instead of ignoring them. The physical exertion of combat training and exercising will help, some. But physical pleasure is a basic need of the human body. Those needs are, like all others, increased in vampires. One way to learn to control your heightened urges is to indulge them, safely."

"So, you, Med-Mage Jensen, are offering me a safe way to indulge my sexual urges?"

His grin was so sultry and wicked that my stomach knotted. "No, I'm your friend, Luca, offering you hot, sweaty, and a little acrobatic, no-strings sex that will satisfy your needs and get rid of some of that excess nervous energy. My soothing power isn't the only way

I can help you calm down."

My brain shut down for a few precious seconds. My body screamed *yes, yes, hell yes*. But there was that small part of me, the part that still wanted Jarrett and no one else, that resisted. "The thing is, Luca, I want you. But I don't know if I want *you* or I just want."

"I understand that. And I'm fine with it. But then, I've been a vampire a couple of hundred years longer than you have. I've had time to come to terms with my body and the fleeting nature of things. Some vampires mate for, well, life. But most don't, yet they still have huge sexual appetites. After a while, you become able to separate the need for love and the need for sex."

My laugh was humorless. "You know, six months ago, that wasn't a problem for me either. Remember, I was raised by a vampire, and when we were teenagers, Pinky had Carly Corsini act as a surrogate aunt for us, for the things he just couldn't talk to little girls about. So the product of two vampires for role models is that we learned that our emotional needs and our physical needs are separate and that we should be smart about both, but not to deny them either. And I never had a problem separating them. But that was before."

"Before you fell in love with Jarrett." Luca's tone was flat.

"Yes," I said, feeling a weight roll off me as I admitted it out loud for the first time. "And I know I need to put that behind me. But..."

"You're not ready," he said softly.

"No. I'm not," I said with a shake of my head.

He smiled sweetly and held up his hands. "That's okay. No pressure. But when you are ready, I'm first in line."

My stomach did a flip-flop. "Thanks, Luca."

"Anything for you, baby girl," he said with a wink.

Fourteen
Anya

PINKY CAME TO VISIT THE NEXT DAY, AS USUAL, AND we worked on meditation techniques that were supposed to help me control my anger and other emotions. It wasn't working, but I pretended it was. I didn't want to fight with him again. When he asked about the memory regression, I told him I was thinking about it. That was a lie. I had zero intentions of putting myself through that. But I was thinking about the other things he'd said, as well as all I'd discussed with Luca, so I didn't feel very guilty about the lie.

It had taken me all night and most of the day to decide what to do next, but as soon as Pinky left, I scryed Sam and filled him in on the plan I had concocted. It took another half a day to hear back from him on whether I'd be allowed to put my plan in action.

I was finishing up the skirt I'd been working on a couple of days before when my scry crystal buzzed. Jumping up, I went across the room to the desk, touching the crystal to activate it. The stone clouded and then cleared, Sam's face appearing.

"Sam, hi! What did they say?" I asked excitedly.

Sam laughed. "You're worse about beating around the bush than your sister."

I grinned, my cheeks heating slightly. "Sorry. I'm just anxious to know if I can get started, or if I have to come up with another plan."

"Put away your planning tools. They said yes."

I squealed.

Sam held up a hand. "But with caveats."

Deflated, I dropped into the desk chair. "What restrictions are they placing on me?" I asked, feeling my victory slip away.

"Nothing you can't overcome, I think. The High Tribunal will allow you to train on your own, and they will allow you to test to become a City Guard Cadet. However, you won't be taking the standard tests. The High Tribunal will devise a series of psychological and physical tests to be administered by a psych-mage and a vampire combat expert of their choosing. They will sit in on the final combat test. If you receive a less-than-stellar rating on any of the tests, or lose your temper even once, you will be denied entry. And no further considerations will be made. You will not be allowed to re-apply for cadet training again until after your tenth anniversary as a vampire."

I sighed in relief. "That's not bad. About what I expected. I knew they would want to administer the tests themselves."

Sam didn't look as relieved. "It's not going to be anything like a regular entry test, Anya. They are going to put you through some tough shit, especially in the psych exams. They are going to try to provoke you at every opportunity. I expect it to be much like how they test for entry to Special Forces units. Don't underestimate their sneakiness. They'll be trying to prove you aren't fit for duty as a guard."

I took a deep breath. "Okay, that's no problem. I know this going in, so I'll just take a little longer to train. I still have nine months before my year of incarceration is up. They'd probably be more likely to consider me at the end of my yearling status, anyway.

On the screen, Sam's eyebrows knitted together and his lips pursed in a way that told me he had bad news.

"What?" I asked.

"That is the other caveat. They are giving you twelve weeks. Your test date has already been set for three months from today."

I stared at him.

Shaking his head, he said, "I told you, they will be looking for every excuse to deny you. You are a special case, and they don't want to set precedent."

I took a deep breath, hearing Luca's voice in my head. *You don't take no for an answer.* "It's okay, Sam. I got this. I can do it," I said, hoping I sounded more sure of myself than I felt.

Sam smiled. "I have no doubt. Now, for my stipulations."

I groaned. "Sam."

"My custody, my building, my rules."

"Fine, lay them on me." I huffed out a breath, knowing I sounded like a bratty kid.

"I'll be allotting a training room on the twelfth floor for your exclusive use for the next three months. You will have twenty-four-hour access, providing you have your guard with you."

"Of course." I couldn't go anywhere without a guard, not even down to the bathing room to take a bath.

"You are not to spar with your guards, but you will need to spar, so I'll send down a list of Blades who will probably be willing. Vampires only. You'll have to work around their schedules, but they will be paid for their time training with you. Since this is a part of your vampire rehab, and the High Tribunal has made the Nash

City Blades responsible for that, your sparring partners will be paid for by the Blades."

I laughed. "Okay, sounds good."

"You'll need a trainer though. I'll send down a list of Blades who would be good for the position and can be re-assigned to you full time. Again, paid for. You can choose who to speak with and let them decide if they want to take on the job."

I cocked my head to the side. "I actually have a trainer in mind, but she's not on active duty. Will the Blades still pay her?"

Sam closed his eyes and shook his head, laughing. "I don't know why I expected anything different." He opened his eyes. "You get Fiona to agree to train you and she'll get paid, hazard pay."

I grinned. "Thanks, Sam."

"You're welcome," he said. The screen went cloudy, and then cleared back to blank stone.

I sat there for a long moment. Twelve weeks wasn't long at all. I realized I needed to get started.

Hopping up, I went to the door, opened it, and popped my head into the guard's sitting room. "Hiya."

The startled guard dropped his book on the sofa where he'd been lounging. "Can I help you, Miss Moon?" he asked.

He was a little under six feet tall with a broad, stocky build. His sandy-blond hair was cut short on the sides with the shaggy top falling loosely over his forehead, just short enough not to get in his sky-blue eyes.

"Yeah, you can. What was your name again?" I asked, grinning to cover my shame that the 'again' part was completely unnecessary. I'd never asked before, and if he'd told me when we were first introduced, I'd completely tuned it out.

"Reece," he said, his tone confused.

"Right, Reece. Do you know where I can get some crates?" I pulled the door open to show the stacks of clothes lined up against the wall. "I need to pack these up."

He thought a moment, and then said. "I'm sure they have some in the storage warehouse downstairs. I can scry down and have some brought up."

"Great," I said. "And can you get access to a wagon? Or even a large handcart would do, I think. Something big enough to carry the crates a few blocks."

He cocked his head to the side, curiosity and amazement clear on his face. "That shouldn't be a problem. Are we going out, ma'am?"

"Please, call me Anya. Not ma'am. And yes, Reece, we are going out. At the crack of dusk if we can get this stuff packed and loaded in time."

Reece grinned. "I'll scry the warehouse right away, Anya."

It took Reece and me a little over an hour to sort the clothes out into type and pack them into the crates. A little after dusk, we carried the crates down to a small wagon hitched to a horse from the Blades' stables. The trip to Pinky's Pub was short, just a few blocks to the front door, but it was still a bit nerve wracking. I hadn't been outside of the Blades building in three months.

I'd been gradually getting acclimated to my overactive senses, but the controlled environment of my room, and even the halls of the Blades' building, hadn't prepared me for the sensory onslaught that blasted me when I stepped out onto the sidewalk. The early evening air was warm and damp with the scents of the city—a combination of dirt, concrete, animal, and human with faint hits of green all mixed with a general fishiness coming from the river. I coughed for a second or two before I got used to it, putting my hands over my ears as the cacophony of city sounds assaulted my ears. Again, it took me a few seconds to adjust. The good thing about being a vampire was that even though my senses were now over-developed, so was my reaction time. In the first few weeks, my body was still re-building, but once that process was complete, my ability to adjust to external stimuli had increased. If only my emotions were that easy to adjust.

I had to shoo a rickshaw out of the spot in front of Pinky's Pub so we could pull the wagon in. Once Reece had tied the horse to one of the hitching posts, we both grabbed boxes and went in. I had to use my key to open the front door because the pub wasn't open yet, but when we went inside, Pinky was already behind the bar, getting things set up. He looked up when we walked in. He flashed me a welcoming grin, but he didn't look surprised. "River and Farrah are upstairs. Are there more boxes?"

Setting my crate on the bar, I leaned over and kissed his cheek. "Several."

"Glad to see you," he said, tweaking my nose before heading outside.

I went upstairs, Reece on my heels, and found River and Farrah sitting at the kitchen table in our apartment eating what smelled like vegetable stew.

"Smells amazing, Rivs," I said, plopping the crate down on the counter.

River jumped up. "Anya!"

She grabbed me and pulled me close in an enthusiastic hug, releasing me so Farrah could do the same. Then the cycle repeated. By the time I'd hugged each of them three times, we were all laughing.

"Okay, okay, you're going to hug me to death," I said, putting my hands up.

"Sorry," River said, not sounding the least little bit

repentant. "We are just excited to see you. It's been a long time, sister."

A twinge of guilt shot through me. "Yeah, about that…"

Farrah quickly cut me off. "No need to explain. I imagine that with all you've gone through, you haven't really wanted to socialize."

I remembered what Pinky told me about Farrah not being able to leave the pub, and the twinge of guilt grew into a giant guilt boulder in the pit of my stomach. Yet from her wavering smile and the uncertainty glittering in her eyes, I knew it was best not to mention that right now.

"Yeah well, I've had Reece to keep me company," I said, jerking my head towards my guard who was standing in the doorway, still holding the crate he'd carried up.

River's eyes widened as if just noticing him. "Oh, please come set that down. So sorry to be so rude."

It was hard to keep a straight face, but somehow, I managed not to snicker. "Oh, sorry. Reece is my guard. Reece, this is my sister River and my good friend Farrah Purcell."

Reece set the crate down on the floor. "Nice to meet you."

"Nice to meet you," Farrah said, smiling. I was glad to see that her anxiety about going outside didn't carry over to meeting new people. But then, she was working in the pub every night, Pinky had told me, so she must be doing well on that front.

River pulled a chair out from the table. "Welcome to our home, Reece. Can I get you a bowl of stew?"

Reece fidgeted for a moment, clearly wanting some of the delicious-smelling concoction, but not sure of the protocol. But after a moment, he seemed to throw caution to the wind. "I'd love a bowl, but first, I need to bring the rest of the boxes up. You'll stay right here?" The last sentence was delivered with a look that beseeched me not to make his job difficult.

"Go." I laughed. "My sister won't let me escape."

Reece flashed me a prize-winning grin, then turned and headed downstairs.

"Wow, he is really cute," River said the moment Reece was out the door.

"Yep. And he has vampire hearing." I laughed as River's pale cheeks flamed red. Farrah giggled too, but covered it with a cough when River shot her a dirty look.

"So, what did you bring us?" River asked, averting attention away from her embarrassment.

"I'll tell you after I have a huge bowl of that veggie stew. I've missed your cooking, Rivs."

Farrah resumed her seat at the table while River went about fixing two bowls of stew. "I have some goat blood in the stasis cabinet if you want."

"Nah, just the stew is fine," I said, digging in.

Pinky and Reece brought up the rest of the boxes then Pinky sat and talked with us while we ate. Conversation was light and pleasant, and once dinner was done, Pinky and Reece went down to the pub, leaving me with two curious women.

"Okay, I can't stand it anymore. What's in the boxes?" Farrah said once the three of us had cleared away the dinner dishes.

I grabbed one of the crates and put it on the table. "Before I open this, I want to set down some ground rules."

The confusion on their faces was comical.

"If there are fluffy bunnies in there, we're keeping them all," River said. "And we're not cooking them."

I laughed so hard I snorted. "No, not fluffy bunnies. Okay, so the first rule is, you have to do everything I say regarding what's in these boxes. Especially you, Farrah. I mean it."

"Um, okay," Farrah replied in a wary tone.

"You too, River."

She rolled her eyes. "Okay. Whatever you say. What's in the darned boxes?"

I opened the crate and pulled out a stack of dresses. "Clothes. Lots and lots of clothes."

They just stared at me.

"Those are the clothes you made with the fabric I've been sending you?" River asked.

"Yep. Now, rule number two. Farrah, you are to go through these clothes and pick out any and all of them you like and want to keep. They should fit you. Same goes for you, too, Rivs. There might be a skirt or two you like."

"Oh, Anya, I can't..." Farrah started.

I tossed up a hand, cutting her off. "Nope. Shut it. What was the first rule?"

"Okay, okay." She laughed, her eyes sparkling. She grabbed another box and started pulling out the clothes. "Wow, these are amazing, Anya."

I couldn't help the pride that welled in my chest. I had always been pretty good at designing and sewing my own clothes, but over the past few months, the constant practice had improved my skills. I enjoyed it, but I couldn't say I was going to miss it. Sewing was a hobby, a way to relax, but it was not what I wanted to do with the rest of my nearly eternal life.

"Thanks. Do you think they are good enough to sell at the market?" I asked, though I knew the answer. I didn't think it was vain to know the value of your own craftsmanship. And mine was good. Some of the pieces even had decorative embroidery, thanks to so many sleepless days and nights.

"Absolutely. I could put them in my stall if you like.

Or I can help you find a local shop or traveling merchant to sell to, at a discounted price, of course."

"I'll let you decide that. Your stall would be great, but not if it's going to be a hassle to find space, especially since you specialize in herbs and vegetables."

River shrugged. "Space won't be a problem, but we'll have to test whether people who visit my stall will pay attention to the clothes. If not, we may have to sell them to another merchant. Any ideas on pricing?"

"I'd like to try to make back a little of the money I spent on fabric, if possible."

Farrah held up a leather corset. "That shouldn't be hard, even at wholesale pricing. Any one of these pieces are worth three times what you paid for the fabric, and some even more than that."

"That's what I thought. So, like I said, please take whatever you want out first. Then, because you know clothes, I'd like you to set the prices. And River, you have to promise not to give the clothes away. Stick to the pricing guidelines Farrah gives you."

River's face went pale with horror. "I would never cheat you."

I patted her arm. "I know you wouldn't. But it wouldn't be me you'd cheat. It would be you and Farrah."

"Us?" they asked in unison.

"Yes. Anything you make back over the cost of fabric,

I'd like for you and Farrah to split between you. Then, if you want to give your share away to the needy, you can feel free." I grinned at her.

"Oh, I couldn't take half the money," Farrah said.

"You can, and you will. You'll be helping River by working out retail and wholesale prices for each piece. And there are hundreds of items. You guys will have a nice little business going. You'll earn every penny. But I still want you to keep some for yourself," I said. Then, I remembered something else. "Oh, and go through my closet. Anything in there you want, you can have. And River, whatever is left of those, either sell to a traveling merchant who deals in pre-worn clothes, or take them down to the slums and give them away."

"But what about you?" River asked. "You need clothes."

"Yeah, but my tastes are changing. Pinky brought me my favorite things, and I want to grab a few things before I leave, but I don't need the rest. You know you've been telling me for years that I have too many clothes."

It was true. I was a clotheshorse. My bedroom was packed with twice as many clothes as were in the crates. I would be ashamed, except I'd bought every bit of them with money I made fighting. I'd started when I was eighteen. At first, I'd contributed to the household funds. Until Pinky found out where the money was coming from. He couldn't forbid me from fighting.

Well, he tried, but it didn't work. But he refused to take any of my money from it. So, I bought things for my sisters and indulged in my love of pretty things. Which came in handy when I started working at the pub. The better I looked, the better the tips for the night. It was a win-win.

"Not that I'm objecting to your generosity, but this is pretty over the top, even for you. What do you have up your sleeve?" River asked.

I shook my head. "Nothing. Okay, don't look at me like that. Something, but I can't tell you yet. I have a plan to start a new career, but I need to keep it on the down low for now. I will tell you this much. If my plans go right, I won't be sewing in mass quantities again. So when those clothes are gone, they're gone."

Farrah flashed a mercenary grin. "Limited Edition Anya Moon designs. That'll drive the price up. I know girls from my own neighborhood who would throw money at words like that."

I laughed. "And that's why you are in charge of pricing."

"And marketing," she said, excitement bubbling out from her. "I can hire someone to make some signs for your shop, if that's okay, River."

River's eyes brightened. "That would be excellent. I know an artist who has a stall at the market. He does amazing work. I can have him come over one evening and work out designs with you."

    I sat back and listened to them chatter about plans. I'd done well. It couldn't completely make up for my behavior and for ignoring them for three months, but they seemed happy. And right now, that was all that mattered.

FIFTEEN
Anya

It was full dark. The pub was open and had a good crowd by the time Reece and I left. The streets were starting to get crowded, and it took us a little longer than it should have to get the horse and cart merged into the traffic. By the time we'd looped the block and made it back to the Blades' building, my nerves were on end from the noise of the busy city street. That irked me, as nighttime on Broadway, and in the pub, with people bustling about laughing and talking, had always been my favorite time. But no more. I felt over-sensitive and harried. Yet, I was determined to go back out in it.

"Reece, how long before your shift ends?" I asked once the horse had been turned over to a groom in the stables.

"In about three and a half hours. You have something else you want to do this evening?"

"If you don't mind, I'd like to take a walk over to the Necromancer's Guild."

He gave me a long look, concern etching his face. "Are you sure? It's an awful lot for one day, being out in the prime busy time of the evening. Especially for your first day out."

"Honestly, I am feeling a little nervy. But I can't hide inside forever. I can't get used to stimuli if I'm not exposed to it. What I have to do is pretty important, and it really should be done tonight."

"I understand. Healer Jensen gave us some pills that are supposed to calm and dull the senses for you to take if you are overwhelmed. Would you like one?"

I shook my head. "No. But stick close, and if you feel it's necessary, stick me with that syringe full of tranquilizer you keep in your pocket."

"You know about that, do you?" He laughed.

"I suspected you would have been given something to ensure I didn't get out of hand in public. What do you say? Up for a walk?"

"Let's go," he said, offering me his arm. I laughed and took it, knowing it would make him feel better if I were close to him.

As we left Broadway behind us, the streets were quieter and the sidewalks more sparsely populated, until we reached the riverfront where the crowds were a bit denser. The Necromancer's Guild was situated across the street from the riverfront, though at one time, the river had been several blocks away. The docks were far enough away that only faint sounds drifted on the wind. Many people strolled the sidewalks along this area of the river, watching the boats drift up and down the river.

I used the scry crystal attached to the outside of the building to announce my name to the guard inside. Within minutes, the door was opened, and Reece and I were ushered up several flights of stairs to an apartment on the top floor.

"Will you wait out here while I talk with my sister?" I asked. "I won't be long."

"No problem. Take your time."

I gave him a wavering smile. In the few hours today that I'd actually been speaking to him, I'd come to find that he was a gentle, understanding person. I decided I would have to make more of an effort to be nice to him, and to my other guards.

I stood, staring at the door for an eternity, then took a deep breath and knocked.

The door flew open almost the instant my knuckles hit wood.

"It's about time. I was starting to think I was going

to have to scry Mrs. Gary to have her send a snack up to you so you wouldn't starve while you got up your nerve," Fiona said, a grin of epic proportions plastered across her face.

I rolled my eyes and used my most bored, *oh-puleeze* tone to say, "Oh, don't be a drama queen. I was just appreciating the peace and quiet for a moment. I knew once you opened the door, it would all be gone."

Despite its ear-splitting volume, Fiona's over-the-top laugh was a calming balm to my frayed nerves. As she pulled me into a tight, bone-crushing hug—which was odd since I was the vampire, not her—I was finally able to admit to myself that the anticipation of seeing her was why I had been on edge since leaving Pinky's. This was the moment I'd most wanted and most dreaded for months.

I wrapped my arms around her and hugged her back, savoring her warmth. "I'm sorry I haven't spoken to you in so long," I whispered into her hair.

Fiona leaned back and stared at me, her face full of love. "You have nothing to be sorry about."

She pulled out of my embrace and walked across the room to a row of cabinets. "Can I get you some tea? I don't have any blood, but I can call Mrs. Gary. There's probably some in the Guild's kitchen."

She was nervous, I realized. She had probably been dreading this conversation as long as I had.

"No thanks, I'm good. Is Ian home?" I swept my gaze around the apartment. It was mostly all one room, with the bed at one end, but there was a door leading off to the bathroom. He could also be elsewhere in the building and still be considered 'at home' since he owned it.

"No, he has evening classes tonight. I have one, too. In an hour."

After she poured herself a cup of tea and gripped the mug as if for dear life, she was trying not to fidget. My sister wasn't a nervous person or a coward in any sense, but she wasn't good with emotions, hers or anyone else's.

"That's okay," I said, keeping my own hands rigid at my sides to keep from wringing them. "This won't take long, and I have to get my guard back in time for shift change, anyway."

She eyed me suspiciously. "Okay. What's up, little sis?"

"First, I wanted to say, again, that I'm sorry about how I've acted over the past few months. I've been bratty and self-absorbed, and I'm sorry."

Setting her tea mug down on the counter, she shook her head. "You have nothing to be sorry about. I made a decision about how you would live the rest of your life without consulting you. You have every right to be angry about it. And that's okay. Thing is, I don't care. I wasn't about to lose you. If you being angry is the price I have to pay for you being alive, then so be it. You can even hate me, and that will be okay."

A hot fist of pain lodged in the center of my chest, but I did my best to ignore it. "That's the thing, I don't hate you. You saved my life, and you don't deserve my hatred. Or my anger. Although, I was pretty pissed at you for a long time."

She pulled one shoulder up in a half shrug. "Everyone gets pissed at me at some point. Eventually, they get over it."

Despite myself, I laughed. "I'm over it. But you should know, I wasn't angry with you for saving me. I have always understood why you gave Jarrett the go-ahead to infect me. You couldn't stand to lose me. I don't blame you. In the same situation, I may have done the same thing. But I was angry with you because you took that option away from me. The option not to lose you, I mean. Someday, I'll have to watch both you and River die. And that is why I've kept my distance. The thought of it hurt too much."

"I know."

"But I'm over that now. Mostly. I'm determined not to let more precious moments with my family be stolen from me. I'm trying to channel my anger where it most deserves to be. And that's on the person who is the real villain of this piece, not you, and not even Jarrett."

I could see dark rage slide over Fiona's features.

"The instant I'm off this ridiculous suspension, I'm going after Cora. I will shred her nasty little heart with my bare hands," she spat out, her words full of venom.

"No, you won't," I said, my voice calm.

She shook her head. "Don't worry about me; I can take care of myself."

I took a step closer to her, my hands clenched at my sides. "Let me make myself clear. If you go after Cora, we are no longer sisters."

Fiona's eyes went wide with shock. "Wh...what?"

"I'm no longer the weak little norm girl who can't protect herself."

"Anya, no," Fiona protested. "That's not what I think. I love you. You are my baby sister; it has nothing to do with you being weak. I want Cora dead for what she did to you, to our whole family. We almost lost you, and that is why I want her dead. That's all."

Emotion welled up inside me, threatening to explode out. I had no idea what form the explosion would take, so I clenched my fists harder, the pain of my nails biting into my palm helping me stay in control. "Fiona, I love you. I respect your need to protect me, but I don't need it anymore. You will always be my big sister, but it's time for me to fight my own battles. I understand how you feel, but you need to understand how I feel. Cora is mine. She will die, and I will be the one to kill her."

Fiona's eyes filled with tears. "Anya, you've never killed anyone. I have—it's my job. I can't let you just go after her and kill her. Vampire or not, you could be killed. If you do succeed, I'm afraid of the darkness that could take you over. I know I spout vengeance, and trust me, I feel it. But if I go after her, she will die by the hand of a Blade, not a vengeful sister."

I took several deep breaths and focused on the sharp, burning pain in my palms. This was what I had come here for. "Then train me."

The look of utter confusion on Fiona's face almost made me laugh. "What?"

"Train me." As I said the words, I could feel some of the tension leave my body. "Help me learn how to control my emotions while I'm fighting, so I can convince the tribunal to let me train with the city guard cadets at the academy. Help me convince them not to make me wait for training."

I explained the deal Sam had worked out with the High Tribunal on my behalf and the training rules Sam had put forth.

"Okay, so if your scheme works, you'll become a City Guard by the time your one-year confinement is up. But will you be happy as a guard?" Fiona asked.

I nodded. "Temporarily. Just long enough to convince them to let me take Blade training. You know it's what I've always wanted, but now, it's what I need. Help me train so that I can eventually become a Black Blade Guard, and when the time comes, I'll take down Cora, the right way."

I watched as Fiona mulled things over in her head, and then visibly willed her tears away. "Okay, I'll train you. I'll help you get into the cadet training, but only on the conditions that you don't go after Cora until you have gone through the full Blade training, and that you won't go alone."

"Agreed."

Sixteen
Anya

Two days after I visited Fiona, we started training. It took her those two days to get everything the way she wanted it. First, she inspected the room Sam had reserved for us and had equipment and weapons brought up. Then she took the list of possible sparring partners Sam had given me and contacted them. She set up a rotating schedule so that I was working with three different partners but never twice in a row. Then she set up two separate training schedules. I would be working with her five days a week, three hours a day. Three of those days would include sparring. But I would be training seven days a week, for a total of six hours a day.

Even with my new vampire strength and stamina,

the first week was rough. The exercises and martial art routines Fiona had outlined for me were advanced and intense. The thing was, I wasn't a newbie. Up until three months ago, I had worked out and done similar training exercises five to six days a week. Though, admittedly, not for six hours at a time. The problem was that my body wasn't used to it anymore. My flexibility, my muscle memory of the moves, all gone. Add to that the new reflexes and strength I wasn't quite used to yet, and all the grace I'd once possessed had left me. I stumbled around, fell, and generally felt like a clumsy oaf for days.

But eventually, I started to improve. I worked out for three hours in the early evening with Fiona. Then alone in the quiet hours of the early morning with my guard outside the door, I practiced form and meditation. I was gaining control over both my body and emotions. But not quickly enough. This became apparent halfway into my allotted twelve weeks.

Scorching pain exploded in my jaw as a blow landed squarely on my chin, snapping my head back with such force that I stumbled back and fell on my ass. I scrambled up as my sparring partner of the day, a vampire Blade agent named Jordan, advanced on me. I dodged his next blow and landed one of my own to his solar plexus.

Jordan doubled over, but only to use his momentum to sweep his legs around and under mine. I landed on my ass again. This time, my head slammed into the floor. My vision blurred with pain, and then cleared as a familiar, white-hot rage filled me. I rose and charged at him, a shrill war cry rising from my throat to fill the air. I didn't worry with form or strategy. I just went for his throat, determined to crush the air from his lungs.

He ducked my attack, thrusting his shoulder into my middle and using my own momentum to throw me over his back. I lunged back up almost the instant I hit the ground and attacked again. This time, I leapt at him, and we both tumbled to the ground. But before I could get my hands around his beefy neck, a sharp pain slashed through my left butt cheek and a familiar calming numbness crawled over my body.

Within seconds, my whole body went limp and I started to fall over, but Jordan gripped me, easing me down onto the floor with care. He rolled me onto my back so that I could see Fiona standing over me, one hand on her out-thrust hip, an empty syringe in the other.

"I'm going to let you lay there for an hour until the paralytic portion of the drug wears off. Meditate, have a nap, whatever. We'll have a nice chat when you can talk again," she said, her tone exasperated.

I let out a quiet grunt, the only reply I could manage, then closed my eyes and let the sedative do its job.

"Wake up, Sleeping Beauty." Fiona nudged my shoulder.

I opened my eyes and slammed them shut again as the room spun. Ugh, I really hated this part.

After a long moment, I pulled my eyelid back slowly, relieved to see the room was still. "How long was I out?"

"About an hour and a half," she said, using both my hands to pull me up into a sitting position. I had just enough control over my body to keep from toppling over backward.

I leaned back, stretching my arms out behind me to keep me propped up. "Damn, I'm sorry. Is Jordan okay? Are you okay?"

The details of what happened were fuzzy. They always were after a rage attack. I didn't know if it was because of the adrenaline overdose or the tranquilizers Fiona used.

"Jordan's fine. I'm good. I shot you in the butt. It was fun."

So that was why my butt cheek throbbed. "Glad I could entertain."

Fiona sat down next to me on the floor, crossing her legs in front of her. "Anya, that was the second time you lost control this week."

"I'm getting better. I was going rage-monkey at least four times a week when we first started. It's progress."

"Yes, but not fast enough. You can't risk an episode like that during your tests. You sure as hell can't have something happen like that when training with other cadets. It's no longer a matter of getting you through the test. If I can't be sure you'll be okay in a less-controlled environment than this, I can't sign off on you going through the tests."

I let out a deep sigh. I wasn't surprised. I'd felt something like this coming. She was right; I wasn't improving fast enough. My control was snapping and sending me into red fogs of rage less frequently, but it was still happening. It didn't take much to set me off—pain from a landed blow, a grazing cut when sword fighting, or a well-timed taunt during a sparring match.

It wasn't acceptable. And I had no doubt Fiona reported every bit of my progress, or lack thereof, to Sam. She was a good sister and would do anything for me, but not at the cost of her integrity as a Blade. She wouldn't do something for me if she honestly believed it would put others in danger.

"What do we do?"

She grinned. "We have a sisterly heart to heart about what's bothering you. We talk about your abduction and Cora. And we talk about Jarrett."

My heart did a back flip in my chest at the mention of his name, and then my stomach started to ache. "I don't see how that can help. I don't really want..."

"Too bad. Look, you know I'm the last one to want to get all touchy-feely and talk about feelings and emotional stuff. But I'm getting paid to do a job, and that's to get you ready for your tribunal tests. Right now, you are not ready. And at this rate, you are not going to get ready. Something has to change."

I knew she was right, but I didn't want to do this. I really, really didn't want to do this. Like, I'd rather have my fingernails pulled out one by one than have this talk.

But Fiona was relentless. "As your trainer, I see something holding you back and making you dangerous. But as your sister, I know something is hurting you. You need to talk about it because neither your sister nor your trainer is going away. I'm not letting go of this."

I sagged in defeat. "Okay, but really, there's nothing to talk about. I can't remember anything about Cora at all. I don't remember the kidnapping, her holding me captive, anything."

"Okay. So we talk about something you do remember. Tell me what happened between you and Jarrett."

Could I do that? Could I tell her what happened in that hospital room? I spent every waking moment of the past several months trying not to think about it, and now I had to talk about it? I didn't know if I could. Because if I did, it would mean having to put words to the most awful thing about everything that had happened. I would have to give voice to the thing that cut my soul deeper than anything Cora did to me.

"He abandoned me." The moment I said it, something broke inside me. A hard shudder started deep inside my core and worked its way out little by little until my whole body shook.

Fiona's voice was oddly soothing when she replied, "But honey, you told him to leave."

"I didn't mean it," I said, my voice so ragged with emotion I started coughing.

Fiona wrapped one arm around me and drew me to her. "Shhh. Don't speak. Just let it out. We'll talk about it in a minute; you just let it all out first."

Hot tears gushed out of my eyes and streamed down my face as I cried—no, sobbed—like I never had before in my life. It was loud, wet, and snotty.

This wasn't like all the times I'd cried recently to release tension and frustration. No, this was what lay behind all the frustration, confusion, anger, and pain I'd been dealing with over the past few months. This was the grief that fueled every tantrum, every snap in control, and every sleepless night. And it hurt to the very center of my being.

We sat like that for an eternity. I cried while Fiona rocked me in her arms, my head on her chest, and she rubbed my back in circles the way Pinky always had when we were sick as children.

After I wasn't sure how long, my tears finally dried up. It was as if my very insides were dry and dusty. My face felt hot and swollen and my head throbbed.

"All done?" Fiona asked, her voice soft and quiet.

I sniffed and sat up. "Yeah, I think so."

"Here, wipe your face."

The damp cloth she handed me was cool against my skin and soothed my swollen eyelids. When I was done, she handed me a glass of cold water. "Drink this, it will help."

I did as I was told, draining every last drop of water before I realized Fiona hadn't moved for as long as I'd been crying, and there were no water outlets in the training room. "Where did you get these?"

"Reece fetched them. He heard you crying from outside. It seems he has even more experience with sobbing sisters than I do."

"How embarrassing," I said.

Fiona sighed, shaking her head. "I don't think you have anything to be embarrassed about. One of the perks of living with an academic is they research everything. Ian has helped me learn what a body goes through after being infected with N-V. I've learned that while your underlying emotional issues are your own, your reactions to them are really quite normal. And being a vampire, I'm sure Reece feels the same."

"I guess," I said, not feeling a bit better about sobbing like a crazed toddler.

"Are you ready to talk about it?"

I nodded. "Yes. I think so."

There really was no use in putting it off any more. I was never going to get control of my emotions if I couldn't face them head on.

Fiona took one of my hands in hers. "Okay. Let's see, where to start? You said you didn't mean it when you told Jarrett to leave. Then why did you say it?"

I forced myself to think about that day in the hospital. How happy I was to see Jarrett, and then how incredibly pissed I was just moments later. "I was angry at him."

"Okay, that's a start. Why were you angry? Because he's the reason you are a vampire?"

I gave my sister my best get-real look. "Really, Fiona? That's what you think of me? He saved my life. Of course I wasn't mad about that."

"Then why?" she asked.

"Because he doesn't love me," I said, hoping to keep it at that.

"Did Jarrett tell you he doesn't love you?"

I shook my head. "No. But he didn't say he loved

me, so it's the same thing."

Fiona dropped my hand. "Anya, you're talking in incomplete sentences. You're not making a lick of sense."

I blew out a breath. There was no getting around discussing this. "When Jarrett came to visit me after I woke up in the hospital, he asked me to marry him. But he didn't tell me he loved me. He just kept talking about taking care of me and making sure I wasn't alone. He felt guilty."

"That fucking idiot."

And with those three words, everything that had been sideways for so long seemed to snap into place. I laughed. Actually laughed. "I know, right?"

Fiona's expression was full of commiseration, but not pity. "But you loved him. You still love him?"

"Yes. Since almost the beginning. And I was okay with that. I knew it could never go anywhere, and I was okay. I didn't expect him to love me back. But when he first said the words—*will you marry me*—I thought, well, I don't know what I thought or felt. Everything was still a jumbled mess. But I know I had hope. I mean, no way he would have asked me to be legally bound to him indefinitely if he didn't love me, at least a little. And I think even if he hadn't said the word love, I still would have said yes. But then he started talking about how it was the responsible thing to do. And I just got pissed. I couldn't help it. My hormones were in overdrive as it was."

Fiona nodded sympathetically. "I think any woman would have been outraged at his stupidity, crazy body changes or not. I would have punched him in the neck."

I laughed. "I would have too, except at that moment I was still too weak to lift my arms more than a few inches."

"Well, for what it's worth, I think Jarrett really does care about you."

I wondered if she was right. "Maybe. I would hope that after everything, he'd had some sort of feelings for me. But he didn't. The second the tribunal was over and he was acquitted, he left town. He didn't even say goodbye."

I could feel the pain bubbling up in the pit of my stomach, but I refused to give over to it again.

"He was sent off on a mission, but he should have let you know what was happening. He should have said goodbye," Fiona said. "I'm not excusing him, but I think he was only trying to do what he thought was right. It was stupid and he needs to be smacked around, but he meant well."

"That doesn't really make it hurt any less."

"I know, An. I know, and I'm sorry."

"It's okay." It wasn't, not by a long shot. Except it was closer to being okay than it had been three hours ago. And when I said the next words, for the first time,

I almost believed them. "I'll get over it."

"I know you will," Fiona said, standing up and moving around the room, putting away the equipment we'd used during training. "But how quickly you get past it is what concerns me. I think you need to make an appointment with Psych-Mage Misra and undergo the memory regression therapy."

Still feeling shaky in my muscles from the sedative, I didn't get up to help her clean the room. Instead, I fell back onto the floor with an exasperated huff. "You've been talking to Pinky."

"Yes, of course I have. But actually, this is my opinion based on my conversations with Misra. And I don't have to turn around to know you are glaring at me, so stop it. As your trainer, it is my duty to confer on your mental health with your psych-mage. She thinks being able to face whatever happened when Cora kidnapped you will help you move past it. I agree with her. Avoiding things never help."

I barked out a sharp laugh and stood. "That's rich, coming from the queen of emotional-issue avoidance."

She whirled to face me. "Yeah, and look where it got me. I nearly died from getting my life energy sucked out by a gooey monster, not to mention almost losing the love of my life because I was too stubborn to face my feelings about my mother. Do you really want to let things eat away at you like that? If you want to pass that test, if you want to become a Blade, and most importantly, if you want to take on Cora without getting dead first, you can't afford to keep avoiding it. It's not avoiding you. It's festering, giving you nightmares. Yeah, I know about the nightmares. What happened while Cora had you, what happened on that balloon, is going to keep haunting your subconscious until you remember it and face it head on."

I wanted to argue. I wanted to fight. I wanted to tell her she was wrong. But she wasn't, and I knew it.

"Okay," I said. "I'm not making any promises, but I'll think about it. And I really mean it. Not like when I tell Pinky I'll think about it."

My sister laughed. Walking over to me, she wrapped me in a tight hug. When she let me go, she said, "I think we should take the rest of the week off."

"I can't afford a week off," I said, balking.

"At this point, you can't afford not to. We had four more training sessions scheduled this week. You can do your form and meditation training, but no more combat, no more sparring. You need to think seriously and quickly about the memory regression. We'll start fresh next week."

I was reluctant to agree, but I knew she was right. In the end, I said, "Okay. I'm exhausted now anyway."

I felt oddly better, but completely wrung out. I wasn't convinced the fatigue setting deep into my bones had anything to do with the dose of tranquilizer Fiona had shot into my ass earlier.

"Yes, you should get some rest."

I started walking towards the door.

"Oh, wait. There is one other thing I think will help you get some control that I'd like you to consider."

A sense of dread rolled over me. I had a feeling I knew what she was going to say. When I turned her way, her expression told me I was right.

"Oh, no, not you too. Why is everyone so concerned about my sex life?"

She grinned. "I'm just concerned. I did a lot of reading, and let me tell you, the things female vampires have to deal with... It sounds both annoying and fun."

"Mostly, it's annoying as fuck," I deadpanned.

"Wait, who else has talked to you about this?"

I made a face. "Pinky and Luca."

She mirrored my chagrin. "Awkward. Well, Pinky kinda had to discuss it with you, it's part of his job, both as your guardian and your dad. And Luca is a healer, so of course he would discuss it with you." She paused, her eyes widening as the truth dawned on her. "Or was he offering to help you out with the situation?"

"Yep."

Fiona let out a hoot of laughter. "And why haven't you thrown down that gorgeous hunk and had your wicked vampire way with him?"

I just stared at her.

Her face fell. "Oh. Yeah. Jarrett. Are you still holding out hope for the two of you?"

I shook my head. "No, of course not. It's just, I love him, and I'm still pissed at him. And I feel abandoned and betrayed. I mean, it's all an idiotic emotional jumble. No matter how attracted I am to Luca, and well, you've read about the hormones. I have jumped him. But I stopped because it just felt weird. He's not Jarrett."

"Wow, heavy. Did you tell Luca what the problem was?"

I let out a snort. "That's the thing. I didn't have to. He just knew. And he's totally okay with it. I mean, if I wanted to jump his bones while imagining Jarrett, he says he would be fine. Because of *my health*."

Fiona grimaced. "Ugh. That's almost as bad as "responsibility". I don't blame you. I mean, I couldn't imagine trying to be with someone other than Ian. But really, you should try. Maybe you can find someone else to have some stress relieving, hot monkey sex with."

I admitted yet another revelation to my sister that I hadn't wanted to admit. "The thing is, I know Luca wants me. It's not all health or responsibility to him. And if I'm honest, if I were going to have stress relieving, hot monkey sex with anyone, I'd want it to be Luca. I just don't know how to put Jarrett behind me."

Fiona frowned. "I don't know either, sweetie. That's something else you should think about this week."

Seventeen
Anya

Feeling utterly destroyed, I stumbled back to my room. Foregoing my usual after training soak in the bathing room, I instead fell onto my bed. And then the most amazing thing happened. I slept, and it wasn't the two hours of fitful sleep filled with elusive, unremembered dreams that had plagued me for months.

When I woke up, the clock beside my bed said I'd slept for nearly eighteen hours. I'd missed my early morning training and meditation session, my psychmage appointment, my medical checkup with Luca, and Pinky's daily visit. At least I had a few hours before today's training session with Fiona.

As I climbed out of bed, I remembered Fiona had

canceled our training for the next four days. I thought briefly about crawling back into bed, but then I looked down and realized I still had on my training clothes, right down to my boots. And I stank something awful. I needed a change of clothes, preceded by a long soak in hot, scented, bubble-laden water. But my number-one priority was food. My stomach growled its agreement to that thought.

I shuffled into the sitting room and stopped dead in my tracks. Pinky was lounging on the sofa, reading a book. He looked up and grinned at me.

"Hiya, sleepyhead. How are you feeling?"

"Confused. Why are you here? Oh, wait, don't tell me. Fiona called you," I said, stomping over to the stasis cabinet and grabbing a bottle of blood. I held it out to Pinky in a grudging offer.

He waved it away. "No thanks, I'm good. And no, Fiona didn't scry me. She came by to have a drink. I asked how your training session went, so she told me."

"Argh!" I flopped down on the sofa next to him, barely giving him time to move his feet, and chugged my blood. "Damn it."

"Don't get lippy. She didn't divulge any sisterly confidences. She didn't tell me anything at all except that you'd had another bad day, but she thought you'd made a breakthrough. So no, I did not rush out and come sit by your side."

"Okay. Good. Why are you here then?" I asked, giving him the side-eye.

"Because Misra called and said you missed your appointment. So I came to check on you. I was going to leave, but then I stubbed my toe—have I told you I really hate your furniture arrangement in here? It's super inefficient."

I gave him my best are-you-kidding-me look. "It's a small space; this is the best arrangement. Now what does you stubbing your toe have to do with anything?"

"Well, Miss Sassy-Britches, I'll tell you what my poor bruised toe has to do with things," he replied, giving me his best don't-get-lippy-with-me glare. "You have been a very light sleeper all of your life. I used to put a spell on your room so you wouldn't be woken up by your sisters going to the bathroom. When I stubbed my toe and yelled loud enough for them to hear me in Atlanta, and you didn't wake up, I got a little worried."

I grimaced, chastised. "Oh."

"Yeah, oh. So I scryed Luca. He did a checkup and said you were fine, that your body was catching up on sleep. Even vampires need more sleep than you've been getting. Yes, our bodies can go three to four days without sleep, if absolutely necessary, but it's not wise to do that often. Nor is getting only two to three hours each night for months on end."

I didn't tell him that even that was a bit of over-exaggeration. I usually slept two hours, max, but many nights, I hadn't even managed that.

"I know. I really do. I just haven't been able to sleep. And I just didn't want to take the sedatives Luca offered. I get tranquilized enough during training." I snorted. "I'm really sorry I worried you."

He wrapped his arm around me, pulling me to his chest and dropping a kiss on my cheek. "It's okay. I'm glad you finally got some rest. I knew you'd be annoyed I kept watch over you, but I couldn't leave until I knew you were okay."

I snuggled into him and let him hold me for a while, reveling in how loved and safe I felt, just like when I was a little girl. But eventually, my own stench was just too much for me. "I hate to break up this love fest, but I need to go soak in soapy water for eternity."

"Yeah, you do reek," Pinky said, dodging the sofa cushion I threw at his head.

"Mean," I said with a faux pout as I stomped into my bedroom.

When I returned a few minutes later carrying a clean change of clothes, he said, "I almost forgot. Misra rescheduled your appointment for six in the morning. Do you want me to go with you?"

Fiona really needed to keep her mouth shut. "No, I'm not sure I'm going to do the memory regression. And if I do, I really think I need to do it on my own. As weird as I know it sounds, I just don't know if I could be brave enough if you were there."

He crossed to me and wrapped me in a long, tight hug before releasing me.

"I don't think it's weird. I understand. But promise you'll call if you need me," he said.

"I promise."

He smiled and left, giving a little wave as he went out the door.

I followed him out, my guard behind me as I went to the bathing room down the hall.

I soaked in the large porcelain tub, thinking about life until the water was icy and the bubbles were all gone. To be honest, that was a couple of hours because I kept asking the attendant to add more hot water and soap. But eventually, I couldn't ponder my life any more without going nuts, so I let the tub drain and toweled off.

As I dressed in fresh clothes, I marveled at how smooth my skin was. A weirdly vain thing to think about, I know, but just a few months before, a prolonged soak in the tub like the one I'd had tonight would have made my skin pruney and painful. But my fingertips were as smooth as ever. Actually, all of my skin was clearer, creamier, and looked better than it ever had before. It was also paler, but the color of my lips and eyes and the natural blush of my cheeks were more vibrant. There were definite perks—and I don't mean my boobs, though those were definitely on-point these days—to being a vampire.

And therein was my entire issue, I realized with a jolt. I was a vampire. Something I'd known for months now, yes, but not something I really owned. And I needed to. I needed to accept that "vampire" was a part of who I was now. Not the defining part, but a very important one. Yes, it was something that was forced on me, but there was no going back. And yes, it was a tool I would use to get revenge against Cora, but after that was over, I'd still be a vampire.

As I stood there looking at myself in the steamed-up mirror, I realized I had been trying to keep that part of me separate from the real me. "Vampire" separate from the "Anya" who I had been before. But there was no division. In order to really take control, not just over my emotions and my body, but also over my entire life, I was going to have to accept that fact. No, more than accept it. I had to embrace it.

And I knew, without a doubt, that the only way to do that was to finally face the reason I had this new descriptor of vampire. And that reason wasn't Fiona, Jarrett, or anything they'd done to save my life. It was what had happened to me. What Cora had done to me. I had to face the reason I barely slept, the nightmares that plagued my dreams, yet were just out of my grasp when I awoke.

I had to undergo the memory regression.

I stopped by Luca's office on my way to Healer Misra's office in City Hospital just to say hi. Like Pinky, he offered to go with me for moral support, but I declined. I did think about it a long minute though. I was nervous and really didn't want to do it, despite my earlier resolve. Yet, I knew I had to. And ultimately, I knew I had to do it alone. It wasn't as if Luca could be in the memory with me.

I left Luca as he was getting ready to leave for the day, making my way to Healer Misra's office. The psych-mage had decorated both the outer office where her assistant sat and her inner sanctum in soft creams, yellows, and earth tones. It was subdued and calming.

I was ushered right in, and Healer Misra didn't seem at all surprised when I told her I was ready to do the memory regression. I'd be damned glad when this one-year shit was up so I could get back to having some semblance of privacy and boundaries in my life again.

"I'm going to have you focus on the crystal while I say some spells to help you clear your mind. Then I'll use my power and push some energy through to help you remember. Your mind will go back to the moments you need to remember. You'll verbally describe everything that happens, and when you wake up, you'll remember it all. No matter what happens, you will be safe and unharmed when you awake. Do you understand?"

I nodded wordlessly, settling back on the cushions she provided.

"Are you ready to start?"

No freaking way. "Yes. I'm ready."

I tried to push my anxiety out of my mind as I focused on the large, oval crystal she swung in front of my eyes as she started to chant. A swirling gray fog rose in my brain until it was all I could see.

My head aches and my mouth has a dusty and foul taste. I try to bring my hand to my head, but my arms won't move. I force my eyes open and see I am in an unfamiliar room. The walls are unpainted wood and the floor is concrete. I look down and realize I'm in a wooden chair. My legs are separated and each tied to a leg of the chair, while my arms are pulled back, tied to the back of the chair.

I struggle, trying to pull free, but it's no use. I try to scream, and that's when I realize some sort of cloth has been stuffed in my mouth and tied around my head.

"Boss, the girl's awake," a deep voice says.

I turn my head, seeing an open door and a giant man covered in tattoos sitting at a table.

"Ahh, wonderful. It's almost time for the call."

A tall, thin woman with long, dark red hair walks in.

I make a noise behind the gag.

She smiles sweetly at me. "Do you want to say something? I'll take the gag off if you promise not to scream. No one would hear you, of course, but screeching and wailing can really grate the nerves when one isn't in the proper mood."

I nod my head in agreement. This woman is a nut job.

She waves to the burly guy. "Remove it."

He does, and I cough for a moment before I can speak. "Who are you? Why are you holding me?"

"I'm Cora," she says expectantly. When I show no sign of recognition, annoyance colors her features. "Surely Jarrett has spoken of me."

Ahh, Jarrett. This crazy bitch was somehow connected to Jarrett. That did not surprise me. After centuries of being an assassin, he must have many enemies lurking around.

"You mean Jarrett Campbell? I don't really know him that well," I say, hoping she'll buy the lie. She

clearly doesn't.

"I have to hand it to him. The man definitely has a type—sassy, redheaded barmaid. Sure takes me back a few centuries." *She gets this weird, far-off look in her eyes.*

"Look, lady. If you think kidnapping me will have any effect on Jarrett Campbell, you are wrong. We barely know each other. I'm nothing to him."

She turns her face to me, her green eyes clouded with fury. Her voice full of venom, she spits out, "Of course you're nothing to him. You are nothing more than a substitution. The poor boy is still longing for me, and he'll use whatever is at hand to sate himself while dreaming of his one true love."

I guess she means her. I try to imagine Jarrett and this woman together. I can't. Mainly because I always assumed he was smart enough not to stick his pecker in crazy.

"I'm telling you, Jarrett won't give a flying crap that you are holding me. But my sister will. She's an agent with the Black Blade Guard, and she'll hunt you down if you so much as think about hurting me."

"Oh, how terrifying," *Cora says with cackle. Before I can respond, she waves her hand and the gag is tied back on.*

"It's time," *she says.* "Python, bring the scry crystal in here."

Once the large crystal is in place, Cora activates it. Within a few moments, Jarrett's face fills the screen. I jump and struggle against my binds as Cora makes a plan to meet Jarrett and Fiona. I shake my head so hard I get dizzy, trying to let them know they shouldn't do what she says, but it's no use.

When the screen goes black, Cora turns to me. "I know what you are thinking. You think it's a trap and I plan to kill your boyfriend and sister. But you're wrong. I don't plan to disturb a hair on their heads. It will be much more entertaining to watch them watch you die—your blood splattered everywhere."

Shock and fear slam into me. Oh, no. This is not going to happen. Fiona won't let me die. Jarrett won't let me die. I force myself to stay calm. They will save me.

Cora unties one of my arms and pulls my wrist up to her mouth.

New terror fills me. She's going to bite me. I struggle and pull, screaming behind the gag, but it doesn't seem to faze her a bit.

She runs her tongue over my wrist. "This will numb it up. No need to give you too much unnecessary pain. Yet."

I struggle again to pull my wrist out of her grasp, but she holds it with an iron grip. I can't compete with her vampire strength.

As I watch, she spreads her lips back from her teeth. I see the two retractable fangs, results of the N-V virus, slide down over her canines. Pulling my wrist up to her lips, she presses them down, sinking them deep into my skin. Her saliva effectively numbed the area so there is no pain, but I still gasp at the hard pressure of her fangs in my arm, slicing into the vein.

In my mind, I want to scream, to try to jerk my hand away, but a strange lassitude slips over me. The pressure where her fangs occupied my arm fades. It's replaced by an oddly pleasant tingling. I know it is because of the chemicals in her vampiric saliva, and there is nothing I can do about it. My mind is still clear enough to be enraged, but the rest of me is relaxing, even enjoying the moment. But then, much sooner than I expect, she pulls away.

I'm not sorry she stopped, but I am curious as to why. She couldn't have pulled much blood out of my veins. I'm not the slightest bit lightheaded from blood loss, as I should be.

"Mmmm," she croons, flicking her tongue out to catch a drop of blood oozing from the corner of her mouth. "So delicious, such a rush. I'd take more, but you are so scrumptious, and I don't want to risk not leaving enough blood to splash all over Jarrett's hands. I shouldn't have even risked tasting your sweetness, but there needs to be a bite evident. No one needs to

know all my secrets just yet."

I struggle to speak against the gag, so she reaches over and pulls it down. "You want to say something, my lovely?"

I suck in deep breaths, fighting against the lethargy. "You're wasting your time. I don't care what you think; Jarrett Campbell won't come for me. He's not going to walk into a trap for some girl he barely knows."

I try to keep my voice strong, confident. But I hear the lie in it, and so does she. I know that Jarrett will come for me. He will come for me because he is a Blade, and that is what he does. And he will come for me because my sister is his best friend in the world. He will come for me because he cares about me. And I know that he isn't attracted to me because I look like Cora. The shades of our red hair aren't even close. I'm not naive enough to believe the connection between us is love, at least not on both our parts. But I know he cares deeply about me, and he will come for me for that reason more than any other. I know that as sure as I breathe, and the knowledge bolsters me.

But it also worries me. Jarrett and Fiona both are brash enough to knowingly walk into a trap to try to save me.

"You know, it's almost too bad Jarrett will come for you," Cora croons, straddling my legs with hers and settling down on my lap. She leans in so that her

mouth is so close to my ear I can feel her hot, damp breath as she speaks. "You're blood is very intoxicating. I'd love to take you somewhere more comfortable and take my time sipping from you."

I swallow a whimper as fear and revulsion bubble up inside me. I'm not about to let her see her effect on me. I won't let her win.

"What? No response to that, pretty girl?" She runs her tongue along my ear. I shudder, but Cora mistakes my disgust for something else. "You see, you liked that. And I promise you'd like being used by me. I'd keep you tied to a nice, soft bed, and I'd find more interesting places than your wrist to drink from. It wouldn't take long for you to be begging me to bite you again and again. I'd have you begging for much more than that, too."

To emphasize her meaning, she presses her groin down into mine.

As bile rises in my throat, I gather every ounce of my strength and channel it into pulling my head back. I slam it forward into hers. The head-butt catches her off guard and knocks her backward off my lap. I watch her stumble, not quite falling, and smile despite the pain throbbing in my forehead.

Rage fills her eyes as she stalks over to me.

"You little bitch," she says just before she swings her arm and slams the back of her hand across my

cheek with enough force to send me, chair and all, flying across the room.

Pain explodes in my head, and everything goes blinding white and then black. I'm not sure how long I'm out, and when I wake, my vision is blurry. After a long moment, everything settles back to normal, except the pain radiating from a single point in my cheek. I'm certain she's broken my cheekbone. I'm lying on my side on the dirty, concrete floor, and I realize my hands are free. Well, not free, exactly. The one she bit earlier is still free and the other is tied to the chair, but the chair broke when she knocked me across the room.

I stay as still as possible, pretending to still be knocked out. I listen closely, but I can't hear anything. They must have gone into the other room. Moving slowly, I test my range of motion. The chair piece my arm is tied to is completely severed from the back, but still partially attached to the seat. I bring the tied hand as far forward as I can and try to untie the rope with my free hand. After several tries, the rope finally falls free.

Untying my legs goes quicker with the use of both hands, though I keep my eye on the door to make sure I'm not caught. Once I'm free, I take stock of my situation. The room I am in is empty save the broken chair, a table, and two other chairs. Nothing of real weapon potential against two vampires. There are no windows, only a skylight, and there is no way I can *reach that.*

The only option I have is going through one of the doors set into two separate walls. I know one leads to the main part of the warehouse, and it is where Cora and her lackey came from before. But I'm not sure about the other. It may be nothing more than closet. But if it is a closet, there might be something I can use as a weapon. Of course, it might also be a room full of vampires, but I don't really have any choice but to chance it.

I scramble across the floor as quietly as possible and pull open the door.

Bingo! It's not a closet. It's a toilet. There isn't anything at all useful in the room except the narrow window above the sink. Moving as quickly as I dare, without making noises that will alert the vampires in the next room, I climb onto the sink and try the window. It won't budge.

Hoping it is just locked, I run my hands around the edges, looking for a latch. I find one in the corner and slide it, then try the window again. It takes a moment of hard pushing, but then it slides up with an audible creak. Knowing the vamps had to hear that, I slide through the window, rolling as I hit the ground. I'm up and running as fast as I can go. But it doesn't matter. No matter how fast I am, I can't outrun a vampire. Suddenly, the big, tattooed vamp is in front of me. I open my mouth and start screaming at the top of my lungs, but he slams his fist into my jaw and everything goes black.

This time when I wake up, I'm lying flat on my back and can't move at all. My legs and arms have been wrapped in rope.

"Oh, good. You are finally awake," Cora says, her tone caustic. "Bring her here, Python."

The brawny vamp pulls me up by one arm and drags me over to Cora. She stands and walks over to me, a long, metal pipe in her hand.

"You know something? You are a rude little bitch. I had no intention of giving you unnecessary pain. I even shared with you the euphoria a vampire can provide a nothing little norm like you. But you fight me at every turn. You spit on my hospitality. I think you need a little lesson in humility," Cora says, her voice cold and cruel.

She twirls the pipe around in her hand as cold ice forms in my veins.

"No! Don't, please," I scream around the dirty rag in my mouth, but it comes out in a shrill mumble.

Cora's smile is so sickening sweet I want to throw up when she reaches over and pulls the rag out of my mouth. "I almost forgot to do that. It wouldn't be near as much fun if I couldn't hear you scream and beg."

I clamp my lips together, determined not to play

her twisted little game.

"What? No more pleading? Very well then." She pulls her arm back over her head and then swings down.

Crack.

I can hear the bones pop and shatter as pain explodes in my leg, radiating outward in slivers of icy fire. A shrill, wordless scream shreds through my throat.

"Mmm, that's nice," Cora says. "But I think you can do better."

She switches the pipe to her other hand and twirls it.

I hop on my good leg, falling against Python, who still has a hold on my arm.

"No, no, please," I beg, tears scalding my cheeks. Every bit of pride is gone. "I won't run again. Please."

"That's better," she says with psychotic glee as she swings the pipe into my uninjured leg.

I scream and scream, and I'm sure the pain I feel will never end. I collapse, Python's hands around my arms the only thing keeping me from toppling to the ground. My legs are useless to me.

Cora picks up a glass vial from the table and walks over to where Python is holding me. She grabs a fistful of my hair and jerks my head back. "If you'd just been a good little girl, you could have had this first and not had to endure any of that pesky pain. But no, you had *to be naughty. I shouldn't give this to you now, but I don't have time to sit around and enjoy your whimpering cries. We must be in place before Jarrett and your dear sister arrive."*

She holds the vial of clear, shimmery liquid to my lips, but I press them tight. Not to be deterred, Cora lets go of my hair and pinches my nose closed. I hold on as long as I can until I have to gasp for breath. She pours the liquid in and holds my nose until I have no choice but to swallow the foul-tasting stuff so I can catch another breath.

"Good girl," she says, patting my cheek before walking back to the table.

I open my mouth to—I don't know—cry or scream or something. But then, the pain in my legs fades away. All of my pain fades, and a pleasant, tingly feeling replaces it. Suddenly, everything is nice and fuzzy and sparkly. I sag against the big guy holding me.

"Bring her," Cora said, strolling out the door.

The giant man, Python—what a funny name to have—swings me up over his shoulder.

"Weee."

I bounce against his back, trying to see where we are going, but all I can see is where we've been, and it's too dark for me to even see that. The world kind of slips in and out for me. There are lights and big hot air balloons. I've never been on one of those before.

Are we going for a ride? But my mouth doesn't work, so I can't ask.

Suddenly, I realize we are very high up. I look down and see Fiona, the pretty lights flickering over her face. "Hi, Fee," I say, but no sound comes out of my mouth. I forgot how to talk. I giggle inside my head at that thought. Oh, and there's Jarrett. He's so handsome. I want to go down to hug and kiss him. But my legs don't work anymore. So I just float here while Cora holds me, and she and Jarrett yell things at each other I can't understand. Fiona is yelling too, and she looks so upset. I want to tell her it's all okay. Everything is so nice and floaty; she shouldn't be mad. But then something digs into my neck. Even through the tingles that dance over my body, it hurts. My neck hurts so much. I gasp, but no air comes. I don't know what is happening. I can't see anymore. Everything has gone gray and misty.

The fog faded. Suddenly, I was back in Psych-Mage Misra's office. Every molecule of my body felt like it was shaking. My stomach lurched and I jumped up, trying to get out of the room, needing fresh air. But I made it two steps and stumbled, falling to my knees. I gulped air, trying to steady myself, but it was no use. My stomach lurched again. The healer knelt beside me, shoving a wastebasket under me just as I heaved my guts up.

Eighteen
Anya

I don't remember the journey back to my rooms, whether I walked or was carried by my guard. I don't remember getting undressed or getting into bed, but I must have, because I woke up tucked tightly in and the clock indicated it was several hours after my appointment with the med-mage.

The soft rustle of breath alerted me to the presence of another person in the room. I sat up and looked towards the noise to see someone had pulled one of the chairs from the sitting room into my tiny bedroom. In it, River sat. Or rather, in it, River slept, her knees pulled up to her chest and her head resting on the back of the chair.

I crawled out of the bed and padded over to her.

"Rivs?"

Her head jerked up. "Wha...? Oh, Anya, you're awake."

I laughed. "Yeah, and now you are, too. What are you doing here?"

"Psych-mage Misra scryed Pinky and told him you'd collapsed after your memory regression. She said it was normal, but that you didn't need to be alone."

I groaned. I wasn't sure I was up to a ton of company, though it was good to see River. "Is Pinky here?"

"Nope. He scryed me at the market to meet him here. After, he went to the healer's office and carried you home. He helped me get you into bed, but then I sent him on his way. I told him you wouldn't be happy about anyone being here when you woke up, but that you couldn't send me away. And, if you tried, I'd give you the goo-goo face." She screwed her face up so that her lips pursed, her nose wrinkled, and her eyes looked sad and pleading. It was the face she'd pulled when she was a kid to get whatever she wanted. Pinky called it her goo-goo face because he said it made him go all gooey in the brain.

"Oh no, not the goo-goo face. You can stay." I laughed and dropped a kiss on my sister's forehead, then went to sit on my bed. I still felt a little weak. "You know, I think you may be the smartest one in the family, little sister."

River flashed a grin, stretching out her legs. "You know, I think you may be right."

I laughed yet again, and it felt nice. "But why are you in here? I'm not sick. You could have sat out in the sitting room, or even in the guard's room for company."

River crinkled her nose up again. "Eww, no. I don't like the guard on duty. She is always so sour faced. It's as if she's never had a pleasant thought in her life."

"Yeah, that would be Misty. She thinks being a guard is beneath her and a waste of her considerable talents. One of the other guards said Misty was assigned this job as punishment for a similar attitude about other duties. Apparently, she has a bit of an I'm-better-than-you complex."

River grimaced. "Well, whatever personal struggles she has, she is not fun to be around, so I didn't want to hang out with her. Didn't want to be alone in the sitting room either. Truthfully, it made me feel better to be close to you. But now that you are awake, why don't I go make some tea? We can discuss getting dinner afterward."

"You're not leaving at all tonight, are you?"

She grinned. "Nope. And maybe not tomorrow either."

I wasn't about to argue with her. "Okay, but can you give me a little time? An hour maybe. I need to wake up and process a few things before I can do anything."

She gave me a long, assessing stare, and then smiled her so-sweet smile. "Sure. I'll go down to the cafeteria and see what they are serving tonight."

I quickly shook my head. "No, don't do that. Just chill for a bit while I take a bath and get my head on straight, and then we'll go out to eat. I'm sick of the cafeteria food."

She laughed. "Deal."

A few minutes later, I found myself lounging in a bubble-filled tub, pondering my life for the second time in as many days.

I replayed the memories of Cora in my head over and over. And at first, a hot ball of anxiety formed in the pit of my stomach, but with each replay, the ball dissipated. A cool calmness took its place. As I sat in the warm, scented water, a sense of peace that had eluded me for months started to seep in.

Any doubt I'd had about whether I'd done the right thing by turning Jarrett's proposal down had been washed away by the new memories, as well.

Now I knew without a doubt that he'd only been asking out of guilt. But not for having turned me into a vampire. He felt responsible for me having been in danger. Sure, in a way, it was his fault I'd been put in Cora's crosshairs, but I did believe he hadn't done that on purpose. There was no way he could have known Cora would kidnap me to get to him. All blame for Cora's actions fell on her shoulders. And one day, I would happily sever her head from her shoulders.

I felt like a weight had been lifted off my chest, off my heart. I hadn't realized how much doubt I'd had over my decision. But not just my decision, but also about Jarrett. I'd been so angry with him that I'd really felt like he'd used me. But now I remember that even while facing death, I'd had complete faith in him. Now I realized that faith hadn't been misplaced or unrealistic.

Jarrett was a good man. No, he didn't love me, but he had cared for me as much as a man like him could care about someone. I'd known from the beginning he was a consummate wanderer. It was my own fault I'd ignored that fact. I couldn't put that at his feet.

I couldn't blame him for me falling in love with him. Nor could I blame him for taking me at my word and leaving as soon as an assignment was given to him. And most of all, I couldn't blame him for not loving me back.

But now I had to figure out how to deal with this. I couldn't pine over Jarrett for the rest of my interminably long life. I couldn't live life like that, not without turning into a bitter shrew.

A memory flashed through my mind of Luca talking about his wife and how he'd been able to talk about her without a touch of sadness. How he'd smiled at her memory. When I'd asked him about it, he'd said she lived in a box in his heart. That he put her memories there and only brought them out once in a while. It was how he went on with his life.

That was what I needed to do. Put Jarrett away so I could move on.

Closing my eyes, I pictured Jarrett. I remembered his smile, his touch, and his laugh. Then I imagined a large box, and one by one, I stuffed each of those beautiful, happy memories into it, slammed the lid, and imagined a steel lock clicking shut.

As I opened my eyes, I was surprised to find that the anger and resentment I had felt for him had vanished. All of my negative emotions towards Jarrett were tied up in the fact that I still had feelings for him, still loved him. But that was locked away now.

Briefly, I wondered if I could do the same with the rage I felt at Cora. But I didn't want to. That fury was the only thing keeping me going right now. Without that focus, the goal of hunting her down and killing her, I didn't know if I had the strength to get through the changes happening to my body. As long as I kept a handle on the hate and anger, I could channel it into a purpose that would help keep me sane.

I only knew one way not to let hate control me. And that was to have human connections. I had my sisters back in my life, but they couldn't provide what I needed. Not everything. But first, I needed to do one more thing.

I got out of the tub, dressed, and went back to my room where my sister waited.

"Rivs, I need your help."

River sold mostly herbs and vegetables at her market stall, but she also sold some lotions and cosmetics she made. Half the beauty specialists and stylists in town were her customers. She was the perfect person to help me in my quest for new hair.

She'd recommended a stylist who specialized in cuts and magic-enhanced color treatments designed for vampires. As I had found out by the several inches of length on my hair, vampire hair grew twice as fast.

I was glad River was with me because choosing the stylist hadn't been a problem, but deciding on a cut and color had been excruciating. I'd always kept my copper hair in long layers, but now, I wanted it gone. All chopped off—bald would be okay.

I needed it to be any color other than red. I was making changes, allowing myself to become someone different. Anya, the kick-ass vampire, instead of Anya, the redheaded barmaid.

Luckily, River wouldn't let me shave it bald. Instead, after much debate between the stylist and us, I decided on a short, but feminine cut that was chin length in the front and much shorter in the back. River also refused to let me dye it solid black, saying I would look like a walking corpse. We compromised with black shot through with wide streaks of blue and purple. It wasn't a bad look.

When River and I left the stylist's shop, my canvas shopping bag was bulging with creams, lotions, and shampoos charged with magic to make my hair grow slower and keep my color self-renewing for three months.

"I haven't seen you smile like that in a long time," River said as we walked down the street, shadowed by my ever-present guard.

Putting a hand to my lips, I realized she was right. I was smiling, and I hadn't even realized it. "What can I say? I like being pretty. I'm not too ashamed to admit that there was no way I could have gone through with going completely bald. I am entirely too vain for that."

"It's more than that," she said. "It's like you are, well, not your old self. There's an edge to you that was never there before. But it's like the old you, the real you, has come out of where ever it was hiding."

"I have. I'm sorry I haven't been myself, but I'm back and I'm not going anywhere again. Not like that, at least."

"Good," she said. "Now let's eat; I'm starved."

"Wow, your hair looks amazing. You look amazing," Luca said when he walked in my door two days after my visit to the psych-mage.

"Thanks," I said, glad I'd had time to get myself together before he got here.

After my adventures in hair styling—and several hours of chitchatting—I'd finally convinced River I was fine and she could go home. It had taken me several more hours to get up the nerve to scry Luca. He couldn't come to see me that day after work, so we'd arranged for him to come by after his shift today. I'd spent all day fretting about what to wear and should have had another three hours, but he'd called a while ago to say he was getting off early and would stop by then.

I'd scrambled to get ready and had put the finishing touches on things just as he'd knocked.

He shut the door behind him and stood still, his eyes scanning the room and taking in the scene. The crystal lamps were turned off in favor of dozens of scented candles strewn about the sitting room and bedroom. I was dressed in one of my favorite drop-shouldered lace dresses. A leather corset cinched my waist tight and pushed up my breasts until they threatened to spill out over the delicate lace. And my makeup, so horribly neglected over the past few months, was flawless.

He took in a sharp breath. "Anya, are you trying to seduce me?"

I quirked up one eyebrow. "Depends. Is it working?"

"Oh, yeah," he said, walking towards me.

"Then yes, that is exactly what I'm doing."

In a flash, he was right in front of me. Our mouths were melded together, my breasts flat against his chest, and my arms around his neck. I started unbuttoning his shirt, wanting to run my hand over the hard muscles of his back, when he pulled his mouth away from mine.

"Are you sure about this, Anya? Tell me you're sure." His voice was rough and thick.

"Yes. I'm positive. But first, there's something you should know," I said, pulling away from him so that I could breathe and think.

"I already know. I understand you're still in love with Jarrett. I told you, I'm fine with that. I have no expectations."

"You see, you don't know. I can't deny my feelings for Jarrett, but I can tell you I've put him and our relationship behind me. In a box, so to speak." I winked at him as I said the last. "I'm ready to move on and get on with my life. I can't give any promises about the future, but for now, I'd like you to be a part of that," I said, hoping I didn't sound as nervous as I felt.

I'd rehearsed this little speech a dozen times, and I still wasn't sure it was going right.

"I'd like that, too," he said, a sensual smile quirking up one side of his lips and showing a sexy, kissable dimple in his cheek. He moved as if to kiss me again, but I put my hand on his chest, stopping him.

"The thing is—you *should* have expectations. You should expect that I am with you because I want to be, not because I have an itch to scratch and you are convenient. Because I have expectations of you. I expect you to be with me because you want me and desire me, not because you pity me or want to help me out in my *time of need*."

His eyes darkened. Reaching up, he pushed a strand of hair from my face before letting his hand slide down to rest against the bare skin of my neck. "Are you kidding me? I want you so much I can taste it."

"Good, because I want you, too. No one else, Luca. Just you."

I took his hand and led him to the sofa. When he sat, I straddled him. I stared in his eyes for a long moment before he pulled my head down to his and kissed me with a ferocity I hadn't known he possessed.

I returned the kiss with equal vigor, reveling in the

taste of him, the feel his hands on the bare skin of my legs. Anticipation and need vibrated through me.

Like the last time we'd been in this position, I was aware that this felt nothing like it had with Jarrett. But unlike last time, I was okay with that. This wasn't Jarrett, it was Luca, and it should feel different. I cared about Luca, not in the same way as Jarrett, but the feelings were there, and they were enough. I pushed the last remnants of Jarrett from my mind so that I could be true to my promise and be completely with Luca.

And it was amazing. Once I stopped thinking and gave in to just feeling, my body seemed to ignite. I went wild in Luca's arms. I couldn't get enough of him. There was something uniquely sensual about him, but more than that, my new body was built for sexual pleasure.

Every touch, every brush of his breath, every stroke of his tongue, sent ripples of pleasure coursing through me. Within seconds, I was hotter than I'd ever been before in my life.

"I don't think I can stand a lot of play. I want... I need you, now. I'm ready," I breathed against his neck, grinding my hips down so that I pressed hard against him.

He slid one hand between us, caressing my thigh until he met the barrier of my underwear. Pushing it aside, he slipped one finger in, finding me slick and true to my word.

"Yes, you are. Let's get you out of this first," he said, reaching his other hand around to unlace my corset.

Unlacing it would take forever. I was too impatient to wait. Leaning up, I grasped the corset with both hands and pulled. The leather shredded in my hands. There were definite perks to being a vampire.

Luca laughed. "That works too. But let me deal with my pants. I don't want to walk home naked."

Grinning wickedly, I moved just enough for him to push his pants down. The moment there weren't any layers of clothing separating us, I resumed my position. Reaching between us, I took hold of his thick shaft. It felt so warm and silky in my hand. The way he moaned at my touch made me want to stroke it and make him moan more and more until he came in my hand. But the solid pulse of need between my legs wouldn't allow that. *Later*, I told myself. That would be fun to do later.

The moans we both made as I sank down on him made me glad I'd had River help me do a sound-deafening spell on my rooms. Then I began to move and everything faded except the heat and pressure building inside me. It was as if every single nerve ending in my body was sending pulses of pleasure. Sooner than I thought possible, I dug my nails into Luca's shoulders as an orgasm rocked me.

As the tremors of pleasure subsided, I whispered in his ear, "So that's what sex as a vampire is like, huh? I think I like it."

His laugh was pure sex. "You haven't even begun to taste the pleasures to be had."

He grasped my hips and flipped me sideways so that I was flat on my back and he was over me, still inside me. Bringing his head down, he licked the tip of each of my breasts in turn, and then looked up at me, his eyes smoldering.

"That wasn't even an appetizer," he said as he began to move, and everything went hot and fuzzy again.

I came twice more before Luca carried me to the bedroom. At some point, we paused to eat before resuming our exploration of each other. Eventually, sometime in the late afternoon, we slept.

Nineteen
Anya

The change inside me was as drastic and apparent as my new hairstyle. After a long, energetic day in bed with Luca and despite a full six hours of sleep—a miracle that happened on a regular basis since the memory regression—I was actually almost a little tired the first evening my training with Fiona resumed. But as soon as I started my work out, my adrenaline started pumping and all of my weariness melted away, replaced by the same jazzed-up energy as was usual. Yet, something was different. My thoughts were clearer, my response times better, and my moves more calculated.

Over the next several days, my performance during training improved dramatically. I wanted to blame it all on the fact that Luca was showing up at my door every morning when his shift ended at the hospital and not leaving until time for me to leave for training. But I knew that wasn't all of it. The regular sex was definitely great for my focus, but a lot of my new performance had to do with letting go of any dreams I might have still harbored of reuniting with Jarrett.

I didn't tell Fiona about my emotional breakthrough, but she was smart enough to figure it out on her own. In classic Fiona fashion, not one to shy away from asking what she wanted to know, she brought it up one day while I was warming up, waiting on my sparring partner for the day to arrive.

"You've been in amazing form for the past week. Ever since we had that conversation about Jarrett. What gives? I know it couldn't have just been what I said. So, spill. Did you get horizontal with Luca?" she asked as I was practicing my sword technique.

"Is that your business?" I asked, continuing to focus on the movements of my body and sword.

"I think so," she said, leaning back against the wall.

"I don't."

"Come on, spill it, sister," she said, tossing a balled-up towel at me.

In one fluid movement, I turned my body, swinging my sword and batting it away. "Nice try at distracting me. Now leave me alone so I can concentrate."

Apparently, that was the wrong thing to say.

"Is that what you are going to tell the High Tribunal? To be quiet and let you concentrate? I can guarantee you they will be trying to distract you at every turn."

She walked over and picked up the towel from where it had fallen. Balling it up, she threw it again. It hit me in the back of the head. I ignored it, moving my position just enough so I wouldn't step on it, and continued to thrust and swing my sword.

"I doubt they'll be asking personal questions that aren't any of their business," I said, impressed at my ability to stay focused and calm.

"Don't be so sure," Fiona said, balling up a second towel and tossing it at my head.

I stepped to the side, and it flew past my cheek. Getting into the game of trying to throw me off my stride, Fiona left the room for a moment and came back with a whole stack of towels and washcloths from the washroom down the hall. She began tossing them at me, while continuing to needle me about Luca.

Clearing my mind, I ignored her words and focused on where she was as she moved around the room, while still focusing on the form and technique I'd learned so many years ago during my first years at the academy.

It was fine at first, but after fifteen minutes, I was starting to get annoyed at having towels hit me in the face. Then Fiona had Jenine, my sparring partner for the day, and Reece, my favorite ever-present guard, join in so I was getting bombarded from all sides. I dropped the pretense of keeping up my form completely and just started dodging and swinging at the balls of cloth zooming at my head.

Suddenly, I had enough. I dropped my sword, whirled to face Fiona, threw both my hands up, and screamed, "Enough."

The towel she had just released soared through the air before stopping abruptly when it reached my hands. It fell to the ground.

I stared down at it. "What just happened?"

Fiona took three steps towards me and lobbed another towel at me, catching me square in the face.

"Hey, what the hell?"

"Sorry," she said. "I was checking to see if you had some sort of force field up."

"Of course, I don't." Since becoming a vampire, I had the ability to do small bits of magic, more than I could as a norm. I could activate a normal porta-scry, instead of the extra juiced up one I'd had to use when I was a norm, and Fiona had been teaching me basic, low-level spells. But so far, I hadn't had any specialized power.

"Then how do you explain that towel stopping like it did? I think you put up a force field. Either that or you have telekinesis and can freeze or move objects."

"I don't know. I was just getting annoyed. I wasn't trying to push energy or anything," I said.

Reece cleared his throat. "That is actually how new powers tend to show themselves. It can take a while for your body to adjust to the changes, and so specific powers don't become apparent for months or even years later. Because you don't know what to look for. A specific power is usually brought about by sheer force of will. I discovered my own telekinesis power in much the same way. Except I sent a rack full of bread dough flying at my crotchety boss."

A picture of an angry Reece with his hand in the air and balls of dough flying about his head now stuck in my brain, I laughed. "You were a baker?"

"Pastry chef, in another life. It was a short-lived job, though." One corner of his mouth turned up in a smirk. "For some reason, that was my last day. It was a shame; I was damned good."

"I expect sweet and flaky evidence of these skills," Fiona said, laughing.

"I'll bring something my next guarding shift," Reece said, giving Fiona a mock-bow. He turned to me. "In my case, it was my second day on the job and my boss, the restaurant's head chef, was ranting about something. I remember wanting to shove the dough I had in my hand in his mouth to shut him up. Next thing I know, all the dinner rolls that were on the racks behind me flew off and pelted him. It was nearly a year after my change. It took me a little while to figure out how to trigger it and control it, but now I can do this."

A spear floated off the weapons rack, zoomed around the room twice, and then landed perfectly in the center bullseye of the training dummy in the corner.

Fiona let out a long, low whistle. "Not bad. Was that how your fireball power manifested as well, Jenine?"

My sparring partner shook her head. "No, I was a mage before I was infected. But I've worked with a lot of yearlings over the centuries, and that does seem to be how it usually happens. Even though it's now standard to test for active powers, they can go unnoticed until an emotional response brings them forward."

It seemed rude to ask if she'd worked with yearlings because she'd infected them with N-V or if it had been part of her work with the Blades. I'd learned, in my history of vampirism classes with Pinky, that during the later years of—and for several decades after—the Spanish Inquisition, the Paranorm Council had authorized Blade agents to infect people in order to replenish the ranks of vampires who had been killed. There had even been teams who scouted candidates such as good fighters and mages with useful powers. The target was infected and pressed into the service of the

Blades.

I found my thoughts drifting to Jarrett and wondering, not for the first time, if that was how he'd been changed. I knew he'd been changed around the era that the practice was still legal and in use, but he'd never really talked about his changing, or his recruitment into the Blades.

Damn it, I scolded myself. Apparently, it was going to be a while before I was able to purge Jarrett from my random thoughts completely. But before I could over-analyze why that was, Fiona's voice brought me back to the here and now.

"Okay, Anya, first we need to figure out exactly what it is you did. What were you thinking and feeling?"

I thought for a moment, and then shook my head. "Just that I was getting annoyed and I wanted the towels to stop hitting me. That's not really specific; I could have stopped the towel, or put up some sort of magical guard around myself."

"Let's test it," Jenine suggested.

First, I tried stopping the towels Fiona tossed at me. I concentrated on the towels, telling them to stop with my mind, but nothing worked. When I was frustrated to the point of screaming, I switched to trying to erect a force field around myself, but it wasn't happening. I was ready to give up. I could feel my temper rising like it hadn't in days.

"Give me a minute," I finally said, closing my eyes. "Calm down. Breathe. Nothing can hurt you. You are fine," I murmured to myself, practicing the calming techniques Pinky had been teaching me over the past few months.

"Anya, it worked!" Fiona shrieked, startling away the calm that had settled over me.

I opened my eyes, following the group's gazes to the two towels at my feet that hadn't been there before.

"You were chanting to yourself. I tossed one, and it just fell away from you. Then another. Whatever you were saying did the trick."

After several more tests, we figured out that chanting "nothing can hurt me" seemed to help focus my energy, which erected a barrier around me. It wasn't very wide, things seemed to fall just mere inches from me, but it was strong, deflecting blows without jarring me at all. Fiona gave up the towels in favor of swords, spears, axes, and every other weapon at her disposal.

By the time we finally stopped, six hours later, I was fending off the electric bolts of magic Fiona shot at me from the end of her hanbo, and I no longer had to chant out loud, just in my head. I was sure that with more practice, I'd be able to focus my energy enough to throw up the shield without chanting at all.

The next day when I arrived at the training room, Fiona wasn't alone. A tall, thin boy of around seventeen or eighteen with shaggy black hair and bright green eyes waited with her. He didn't have the alert stillness I had come to recognize in other vampires, so I knew he wasn't a new sparring partner.

"Hi," I said, giving my sister a quizzical look.

"Anya, this is Simon," she said, motioning to the boy, who hooked his chin up in an unenthusiastic acknowledgment of my existence. "Simon's going to help us test your shielding power."

I laughed. "You ran out of things to hit me with yesterday so you're going to start throwing teenage boys at me?"

Rolling her eyes, Fiona laughed. "No, Simon's going to be the one throwing things at you. Balls of magic to be precise."

"You did that yesterday, and it didn't touch my shielding. What can this student—I'm assuming—do that you can't? No offense." I said the last with a look at the boy.

He shrugged. "None taken," he said in that flat, uncaring tone only teenagers seem to be able to pull off.

Fiona shook her head. "Oh, little sister, I was taking it easy on you yesterday. But today is about something else. Simon is a student, but he is very powerful and has excellent control. He can throw energy balls like no one I've ever seen. He almost kicked my ass once."

That brought a grin to the boy's flat features, transforming him into a beautiful creature who probably had to beat the girls off with a stick. "Yeah, I did," he said, smirking.

"Almost," Fiona emphasized with a laugh. "Don't get too big for your britches, boy. I can still take you."

"For now," Simon shot back, a wicked gleam in his eyes.

We started working, first using blunt weapons and then swords to make sure I could recreate my shields. After that, Simon started throwing balls of energy at me. Fiona hadn't been exaggerating; the kid had incredible power and control.

After two solid hours of throwing glowing balls of magic at me, Simon was starting to tire, so we called it a day. But we'd learned quite a bit in a short time. As it had with Fiona's pinpointed energy attacks, my shield seemed to absorb Simon's energy balls when they were thrown from a distance. It was as if the energy melded into my shield, making it stronger. I felt no pain, and only about as much pressure as if someone were gently shoving me. But the closer he moved to me and the more force he put behind the attacks, the harder the shoves became. While the energy still seemed to strengthen my shield so that I didn't have to expend any extra energy to keep it up, I did have to work harder to stay on my feet. Simon even knocked me on my ass twice.

Once Simon left, Fiona said, "I'd like to try you out with some sustained energy blasts from my hanbo tomorrow. See how you hold up to a continuous attack. If my theory holds, your force field should feed on the energy and have no effects. I also want to see if Jenine's fireballs have the same effect, of if they weaken your shield."

"Ooh, fun," I said with zero enthusiasm. "My luck, the shield will disintegrate and I'll get my hair singed."

"Oh, don't be a baby," Fiona said. Her voice turned serious. "Anya, I don't think you should tell the High Tribunal about your shielding ability."

I frowned, my forehead getting all wrinkly. "Don't you think it would be a plus? Something in my favor to show I have control?"

She shook her head. "No, I don't. I think it would be quite the opposite. Your power manifested after you'd gained some emotional control. We are less than two weeks away from the start of your psych tests. We have no idea if those will affect your ability to shield."

I could see where she was going. "And if the tribunal knew about the shield, they'd have the combat testers focus on making it weaken and go down."

"Or making you lose control of it. I want to take one more day to test the limits of your ability, but after that, we need to get back to focusing on your whole training. You need to be able to meld it into your fighting techniques seamlessly or not use it at all," she said.

"Okay, I get that. But how do we keep it a secret? Simon knows about it and so do Jenine and Reece."

"Mum's the word," Reece called to us from the corner where he was lounging on a chair.

"Simon was sworn to secrecy before I even told him what I wanted him to do today, and I trust him. And leave Jenine to me. Technically, she is working under me, so I can order her to keep it to herself," Fiona said.

"You won't have to," Reece replied from his corner. "I've known Jenine a while, and she's a lot like me. We respect the laws and we uphold them, but we don't necessarily trust the tribunals or the Council implicitly. We understand the safety in keeping some things close to the vest."

I wondered what secrets the quick-witted, jovial vampire who had become my friend in the past weeks held, but no way would I butt my nose in and ask. "Okay then, it's settled. Mum's the word on my powers. Now I'm going to take a long, hot bath."

"Got a hot date in the morning?" Fiona asked.

I flashed my best wouldn't-you-like-to-know look and strode out the door, a snickering Reece on my heels.

Twenty
Anya

"Tell me what you know about the vamp I'm fighting," I said to Fiona as I started my pre-fight warm-up stretches. It wasn't something I had to do to avoid injury anymore. But warming up helped me prepare, get in the right frame of mind for a fight. Or so it had when I was a norm, and I'd continued the practice for all of my sparring matches. But today wasn't a training session.

We were in our regular training room so I could prepare, but soon, we would go downstairs to the large gymnasium used by Blade cadets where I would face my final test by the High Tribunal.

"Not much. His name is Kane. I know he's a vampire and he's old—like a lot of centuries before the

Cataclysm old. Sam said he is from the region of the world where many martial arts practices originated, and he is a master at hand-to-hand combat. To me, he doesn't look that scary. He's not very tall or heavily built. Though his muscles are well defined."

One thing I knew from my years in the fight houses was that while the big, burly dudes brought in the highest bets because they looked tough, the small guys with defined arms were the ones to watch out for. They were usually the ones with the most skill.

I took a deep breath. I could do this. I could do this. What if I couldn't do this?

As if hearing my thoughts, Fiona said, "You've got this. You've trained hard, and you've passed all of their psych tests over the past three days. You can beat this guy. You're the best fighter I know."

"Yeah, but you don't know Kane," I said, snorting.

"No, but I know you. And I know what the tribunal is up to. They've done their best to intimidate you, especially with staging this test like a match at a fight house. I don't know what they are thinking inviting an audience." She shook her head. "Yes, I do. They are trying to psych you out. Which means their choice of opponent was made for that reason, too. Don't let them get inside your head."

I tried not to worry, but I couldn't help the nervous quaking in my stomach that threatened to force my breakfast out.

I finished my warm-ups and couldn't find another reason to put off going down and getting things over with. "Okay, I'm ready."

Fiona came over to me and took my hands, staring me in the eye. "You are going to beat this guy to a bloody pulp. You know why? Because you are a bad-ass bitch!"

I snickered, and she smacked me on the arm.

"Don't laugh at me when I'm trying to give you a pep talk."

"Sorry." I snickered again.

She grabbed my head, one hand over each of my ears, and pulled my forehead to hers. "You are tough, you are strong, and you are a stubborn-ass Moon sister. You have got this." She pulled her forehead back and then bumped it into mine. "You. Have. Got. This." Her voice was full of force.

I let her confident energy slip over me. "I've got this."

"You've got this."

"I've got this!" I nearly shouted.

"Okay, now you're ready. Let's go," Fiona said, opening the door and leading the way out. I followed. Reece, who had been waiting outside the door, brought up the rear.

Four rooms the size of my training room could

have fit inside the room the test was being held in. Like where I had been training, there were racks of weapons, training equipment, and heavy bags lining the outer walls. But in the center, a makeshift ring had been set up. Outside the ring, several rows of folding chairs had been set up to one side for spectators. Pinky, River, Sam, and Luca were all seated, along with several Blade agents I'd gotten to know over the past few months, and a few people I didn't know but suspected were representatives of the Nash City government. On the other side was a long table with the three High Tribunal magistrates seated behind it.

Next to the table stood a dark-haired man. He was bare chested with several tattoos crossing his well-muscled torso. His face was set in a grim mask.

Taking a deep breath, I tried to clear my mind. I wouldn't let fear defeat me before I'd even started. Crossing into the ring, I stood in the center.

"Ahh, yes, Miss Moon," the male magistrate said. "You are finally here. We can get started. Basic fight house rules apply; I believe you are familiar with them."

I wanted to wipe the smirk right off this guy's face. He thought he was putting me down, as if I should be ashamed of my past as a brawler. But I wasn't. It was the one thing in my past I longed to be able to go back to.

I smiled the sweetest, brightest smile I had. "Yes,

Your Honor. Quite familiar."

"Good. The match will be ended when one of you is down for a ten count or willingly taps out."

Kane stepped into the ring and stood at attention with his fists in front of him, the muscles on his arms straining under his skin as if trying to burst through.

It took everything I had not to turn and run. Vampire strength was one thing, but muscles like that on a vampire meant heavy-duty attention to keeping them honed. Which spoke not just to his strength, but also to his level of experience. Trying not to show any fear, I backed to the other side of the ring, as was dictated in a formal fight. Then a bell rang and the match started.

The first few seconds, we hopped around the ring, assessing each other. When I thought I had an opening, I thrust my leg out in a fast, hard kick at his middle. He easily caught my heel, twisted it, and flipped me on my face. I hit the floor with a thud.

Well, that was humiliating.

I hopped up and looked for another opening. Soon, we were trading blows. We seemed evenly matched, but I didn't buy it. He was toying with me, and I knew it. But I had something up my sleeve, too. I hadn't put up my shield. Instead, I'd taken every punch and kick he'd landed. He wasn't the only one who could lure someone into a false sense of security.

After a while, he started moving faster and faster. I

couldn't land anything, but his punches and kicks were finding me with super accuracy. I couldn't dodge him. Finally, his heel connected with the side of my head hard enough to knock me to the floor.

This was the moment I'd been waiting for. I stayed down, on my hands and knees with my head bent, until the referee hit five in the ten count. Then I slowly rose, stumbling as if injured.

That was not to say I wasn't hurting for real. I was. My head was pounding, and I was pretty sure he'd cracked a rib. But even though the pain was intense, it didn't hinder my movement or ability to think clearly. And, thanks to my wonderful new N-V-ridden blood and altered DNA, the pain was receding fast. But there was no need for Kane to know that.

I stumbled towards him, my hands up, and when he swung, I didn't block him. But I did throw up my magical shield. The fist to the head that should have knocked me on my ass just bounced away from me, never making contact.

As his face registered confusion, I used his distraction to land a solid right hook to his jaw. From there, I stopped stumbling and pretending to be feeble. I let loose on him with everything I had. It quickly became a matter of who would tire faster. Using magic to keep my shield up ate away at my energy. But pain did the same thing to Kane, and I did my best to deliver as much I could.

He hit the ground and had the ten count started twice, but rose quickly each time. The third time I knocked him down, I stood back, hoping beyond hope he wouldn't get up. I was getting tired, and shield or no shield, one good hit would do me in.

But as the referee reached eight, Kane climbed to his feet. But he was wobbly, and I saw my chance to end it. I lunged at him, swinging, but he grabbed my arm, flipping me over his shoulder. I hit the ground, but I'd grabbed hold of him and took him with me. He sprawled next to me, and I quickly maneuvered to give him a shot to the solar plexus with my elbow. Then I rose over him, my fist pulled back, ready to strike. But his face was slack with pain and fatigue. He tapped on the floor three times.

"The match has ended. Anya Moon is the victor," the referee announced. A cheer went up in the crowd.

I hopped up and stood back, giving Kane room. He stood, bent towards me in a slight bow, then turned and wordlessly left the room.

The three judges stood. The male, the seeming spokesman for the day, said, "We will adjourn for ten minutes."

They turned and followed Kane out.

Exhausted, I sank to my knees.

Fiona, the only person allowed to come to the ring,

was by my side in an instant. She handed me a bottle of water. "Are you okay?"

"Yes," I said, chugging the water. "Just a little tired."

"I imagine you would be. You two have been going at it for nearly two solid hours," she said.

I turned to look at her, my eyes wide with shock. "No way? Really?"

She nodded. "Yeah, it was really intense. You did a wonderful job."

"Thanks," I said. She held her arms out to me and I leaned into her hug, resting my head against her shoulder while I gathered my strength.

We sat like that until the High Tribunal filed back in, then I stood and Fiona went back to sit with Pinky and River.

This time the blonde woman, the vampire magistrate, spoke. First, she droned on about the reason for the tests and the seriousness of upholding the laws regarding N-V infection. "That said," she said, looking me straight in the eye. "Anya Moon, you have shown yourself to be in excellent control of your faculties. Indeed, you have better control than many who have been vampires for decades. Additionally, your fighting skills and other abilities suggest you will make an excellent member of the law enforcement community. You have the approval of the High Tribunal and the Paranorm Council of Elders to join the next class of City Guard cadets."

A cheer went up from the crowd.

The blonde vampire glared at them. "Please hold applause until the end; this is a court proceeding, after all. Now, where was I? Ah, yes. Furthermore, in light of the results of your tests, we no longer feel it is appropriate for you to be under twenty-four-hour guard. You are hereby released from the custody of the Nash City Black Blade Guard under Sam Harrison's supervision and remanded to the custody of your adopted father, Eric Pinkerton, until such time as your yearling status is up."

Another, louder, cheer went up, and I could hear Fiona's voice leading the pack.

This time, the judge just shook her head, and I was sure I saw a smile trying to curve her lips. She banged her gavel on the table.

"This proceeding is over."

The three magistrates rose and filed out of the room.

I stood there, unable to move. I felt as if I'd been body-slammed and the air knocked out of my lungs. I couldn't believe it was over. I'd won.

It would never be completely over until I'd faced down Cora, but at least now, I could move on with that plan, while getting back to some semblance of a real life.

As I stood there trying to catch my breath, I looked up and saw Luca standing near the edge of the ring with Pinky and my sisters. His smile was broad and proud, with a hint of something else behind his eyes.

When we started sleeping together, he said he would be okay with a no-string's arrangement. In the weeks since that first night, he'd said and done nothing to contradict his words. But I knew better. He was already tangled in a mess of strings; I could see it in his eyes. Yet, I knew he'd never tell me. I thought I was okay with using him because he knew he was being used and was fine with it.

But now, I wasn't so sure. The fact was, I enjoyed Luca. I liked being around him, and the sex was pretty great. I didn't think I'd ever feel about anyone the way I'd felt about Jarrett, but perhaps being tangled up with Luca wouldn't be so bad.

Of course, I wouldn't let him stand in the way of my ultimate goal to hunt down Cora. But it would be nice to know he was waiting for me at home.

After I took down Cora, I could work with the local Blades like Fiona. I could have my dream job and come home in the mornings to the care and attention of a good man. I could think of worse ways to spend a lifetime or two.

Luca looked up, saw me staring, and waved, his smile widening. My stomach gave a little lurch. I thought I could get used to seeing that gorgeous face every day. I waved back and went over to join the celebration.

EPILOGUE
Jarrett

THE BUILDINGS OF NASH CITY POPPED UP INTO view over the horizon. A steady pulse of anticipation began to beat in the pit of Jarrett's stomach. He stared out the air-ship window as the city loomed closer and closer.

The flutter in his belly spread through his veins until his entire body was humming. He knew it wasn't just the call of freedom, or the relief at having his sentence commuted and being released from prison two years early. It wasn't his confusion as to why that had happened. It wasn't even his anticipation at having a long, hot shower and sleeping deeply and safely in his bunk aboard The Minnow.

As appealing as all of those things were, they were

not the source of his excitement and agitation. It pulsed in a rhythmic two beat as if it were trying to tell him something, and if he closed his eyes, he could almost hear the syllables. *An-ya. An-ya. An-ya.*

Anya. As the city's skyline crept ever closer, so did Anya.

Jarrett knew she might not want to see him. He'd screwed up monumentally the last time they'd been together. But he'd had three long years to think about what he'd done wrong. He realized now that his fear of opening himself up to her had been his biggest failure.

He loved her, and he should have told her that first thing. Certainly before he'd proposed. If she had still denied him, at least she wouldn't have felt as if his offer had been purely out of guilt. He had been so thick-witted about the whole thing. If Fiona hadn't let slip how her sister had felt in one of the many letters she'd written him over the past few years, he probably never would have realized what a twat he had been.

But now he knew. And he knew his second mistake had been giving up too easily. He'd acted rashly, proposing to her before she'd even had a chance to come to terms with her new life, her new body. In an idiotic moment of hurt pride, he'd taken her rejection as absolute. He'd immediately pulled back and then, in a misguided effort to protect her, had cut off all ties from her. Even to the point of not allowing Fiona tell her he'd been sent to a prison camp.

Though Fiona had never come right out and said so, he was certain Anya had felt he'd rejected her. How could she not? He'd turned her into a vampire, clumsily proposed, then, as far as she knew, rode off into the sunset without a backward glance.

But that was all in the past now, and he'd had three years to come to terms with his mistakes and plan how to fix them. First, the hot shower and night of rest where he didn't have to be on high alert in case someone wanted to attack him. After that, he'd find Anya and tell her he loved her and would for all the days of his endless life. And then she'd probably punch him in the face.

The corners of his mouth quirked up at the thought. He missed his tough, yet fragile ginger.

He had no doubt she would still be angry with him. He knew she might have moved on. A flash of anger surged through him as he remembered the way that med-mage, Luca, had looked at Anya.

It didn't matter. Jarrett wasn't giving up without a fight.

About the Author

June is a geek girl, fat chick, and unrepentant romantic. She writes full time and is both independently and traditionally published. She also works part time running her greeting card company.

When not working, June can be found making jewelry, reading, cooking, or watching geeky movies with her husband and snuggling with her 6...YES 6, furbabies. Notice cleaning wasn't listed...

Acknowledgements

This book has been a labor of love not just by me, but by an entire crew of people working with me, supporting me, and keeping me on track, from my entire publishing team at Crimson Tree, to my tireless street team, the Damsels Not in Distress.

I have to give an extra special thanks to a couple of my street teamers. First to Lauren, who so kindly let me borrow her name for Luca's wife. She may or may not also have crazy hair, a mouth like a sailor, and stinky farts. And to my right-hand Damsel, Amy who always goes above and beyond any time I cajole her into helping me out. She is a beautiful and amazing person, and I'm lucky to have her on my side.

Speaking of above and beyond... I would never get a thing done, both in work and life, without my bestie Sherry Ficklin urging me on, talking me down from my bi-weekly freak-outs, and giving me a good swift kick in the britches when needed.

I also can't forget my mother-in-law who has endured endless hours of listening to me detail which ever book I'm working on, and yet she always manages to seem interested. Of course that pales in comparison to the reason I'm grateful for her every single moment of ever day... giving birth to my wonderful husband.

And with that flawless segue, I'll wrap this up with a mention of the love of my life, the one that is always there for me, who brings me soup and medicine when I'm sick, puts up with my weirdness, and feeds the furbabies... my husband, my Geek Hero.

Printed by Libri Plureos GmbH in Hamburg, Germany